Child Wanted

Renee Andrews

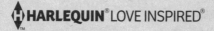

Recycling programs for this product may not exist in your area.

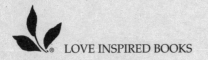

LOVE INSPIRED BOOKS

ISBN-13: 978-0-373-89943-2

Child Wanted

Copyright © 2017 by Renee Andrews

www.Harlequin.com

Printed in U.S.A.

"So, did y'all catch anything, Jerry?" Lindy asked.

"No, ma'am," he said, "but Mr. Ethan said we're going to get some Popsicles anyway."

Her gaze moved from Jerry to Ethan, and he saw a hint of appreciation in her eyes that went straight to his heart.

"Yeah, sometimes those fish do play hide-and-seek," she said, "but I'm hoping they won't play so well the next time."

"Me, too," Jerry said, nibbling the end of his Popsicle.

"I got you a peach one," Ethan said.

"You didn't have to do that," she said. "But thank you."

Jerry glanced at Ethan, and then watched Lindy as she tried hers. "Do you like it, Miss Lindy?"

She nodded. "I like this," she said, giving him a tender smile. "I like this very much."

Ethan watched her, eating his Popsicle and sitting beside his future son, and he knew she wasn't just talking about the Popsicle. She, like Ethan, enjoyed the feeling of sitting on the porch with a little boy, spending time together on a beautiful early summer day.

And he found himself suddenly wondering if what she liked so much about this moment included him.

Renee Andrews spends a lot of time in the gym. No, she isn't working out. Her husband, a former All-American gymnast, owns a gym and coaches gymnastics. Renee is a kidney donor and actively supports organ donation. When she isn't writing, she enjoys traveling with her husband and bragging about their sons, daughters-in-law and grandchildren. For more info on her books or on living donors, visit her website at reneeandrews.com.

Books by Renee Andrews

Love Inspired

Willow's Haven

Family Wanted
Second Chance Father
Child Wanted

Her Valentine Family
Healing Autumn's Heart
Picture Perfect Family
Love Reunited
Heart of a Rancher
Bride Wanted
Yuletide Twins
Mommy Wanted
Small-Town Billionaire
Daddy Wanted

Visit the Author Profile page at Harlequin.com for more titles.

Be kind and compassionate to one another,
forgiving each other, just as in Christ
God forgave you.
                    —*Ephesians* 4:32

This book is dedicated to the ladies who lunch: Connie, Gay, Linda and Marie. Life is so much better when I get to spend time with all of you!

Chapter One

"Jerry, this is Mr. Green."

Ethan Green crouched to eye level with Jerry Flinn as Mrs. Yost, the social worker, introduced the four-year-old boy to the thirty-year-old man. "Hey, Jerry. I've been looking forward to meeting you."

Talk about an understatement. Every day for the past three years, Ethan had prayed for the sandy-haired, freckle-faced child. He was fisting his hands in the fabric of his navy T-shirt as he edged backward, his eyes darting from the social worker to Ethan to the couple that ran the children's home in this tiny town of Claremont, Alabama, where Jerry had been placed merely three days ago.

Ethan recognized the panic, the terror, pushing through his future son's veins. He wanted to run. Or cry. Or both. But he also wanted to be tough. Be strong. Control the fear.

Ethan knew each of these emotions first-hand.

God, please help me know what to do, what to say, to gain his trust.

"Hey Jerry, I got some bread for you and your friends to give the geese." Ethan held up the brown lunch sacks of stale bread that he'd purchased at one of the stores on the town square. He knew the twins belonging to Brodie and Savvy Evans, the couple that ran Willow's Haven, weren't technically Jerry's "friends" yet, since he'd only met Rose and Daisy three days ago, but Ethan wanted him to know that they would be. It was important for Jerry to understand that he would have friends and that he now had people who cared about him in his life.

Like Ethan.

"You got bread for us?" Rose hurried toward Ethan with Daisy at her heels. If their names weren't on their pink and yellow T-shirts, he'd have never been able to tell them apart.

"I sure did." He handed a bag to each girl and then waited for the little boy to approach him. Instead of moving toward Ethan, however, Jerry merely watched Rose and Daisy dart past him, their laughter filling the air as the squawk-ing geese began a rendition of follow the leader, or rather, follow the bread sacks. Rose flung a piece behind her, and several headed for it, then she and Daisy tossed more on the opposite side.

The geese waddled beyond the girls to get to the scattered pieces. And Jerry held his ground, red tennis shoes rooted in place and hands stuffed in the pockets of his jeans.

"Jerry, I got a bag for you, too. Don't you want to feed the geese?"

He looked at the girls and then the sack in Ethan's hand. He slowly nodded.

Ethan said a quick prayer of thanks. "Okay then, here you go." He extended the bag, but Jerry merely looked at it, still not budging.

"I'll put the sack right here." Ethan placed the paper bag on the concrete edge surrounding the three-tiered fountain that designated the center of Claremont's town square. "And then I'm going to sit and watch you feed the geese, okay?"

Jerry's gaze fixed on the bag.

Ethan walked away from the bread and sat on the opposite end of the park bench from the social worker. "You may want to get it soon—" he forced a little laugh "—or those geese may go after it without you."

Daisy giggled from the other side of the fountain. "Yep, go on, Jerry. You need to get your bread and start feeding them before they eat all of ours!"

Jerry shot a glance toward the girls, surrounded by geese, then to his bag, and then to Ethan. Small shoulders lifted as he sought the courage to step toward the sack. Easing closer, he snagged it as if he thought Ethan planned to grab it first, before Jerry had a chance.

Maybe that was the type of thing he was used to, but that wasn't the way things were— not anymore.

"Great." Ethan gave him a thumbs-up. "Now you can feed those hungry geese."

As if his words were an invitation, the geese transferred their focus from the girls to Jerry.

The little boy's blue eyes widened, hinting at obvious fright at the onslaught of the noisy animals.

Ethan knew better than to rush toward the child, so he instead leaned forward on the park bench and spoke soothingly. "It's okay, Jerry. Just toss a few pieces away from you. You can even throw some in the fountain if you want. They'll probably get wet trying to get the bread."

Undeniably frightened, Jerry plunged his fist into the bag, grabbed a handful of bread and flung it into the fountain. As predicted, the geese headed into the splashing water, dipping their heads beneath the surface and wiggling their backsides in an effort to get the sinking and bobbing bits of bread.

Rose and Daisy jumped up and down, clapping and laughing at the spectacle. But Jerry clamped his mouth together. Was he afraid to smile? Had he gotten in trouble for laughing or smiling in the past? He also kept peering toward Ethan and Brodie, the only men near the fountain, as though expecting some sort of reprimand for tossing the bread.

Ethan scrubbed a hand down his face, at a loss for how to handle the situation. As an eighth-grade English teacher, he interacted with adolescents on a daily basis and attempted to provide a fatherly example to the kids in his classes. But he'd never spent a lot of time with four-year-olds, particularly ones who had been so abused that they feared the majority of adults.

Which was exactly why Ethan wanted to adopt Jerry. Every little boy deserved a father he could count on, someone to care for him and protect him. Ethan could do that for Jerry. He wanted to. He'd *prayed* to be able to.

But, in all of his anticipation for how this first meeting would play out, he hadn't considered the extent of the boy's fear.

If Gil Flinn weren't a dead man, Ethan would

have a hard time fighting the impulse to make him pay for the trepidation in his little boy's eyes. And if Melinda Sue Flinn weren't behind bars for killing him, he'd let her know exactly what he thought of a mother who'd stand by and allow her husband to abuse their son.

"He'll need time." Mrs. Yost jotted another note on her tablet and then slid it in the large red bag that appeared to hold enough files for at least twenty children. "He's been through so much, not only with what happened with his birth parents but also another upheaval with his first long-term placement in the system not working out."

Ethan nodded, knowing exactly what she was talking about. He felt even more empathy toward the sad little boy.

"But the good news is," she continued, "based on his past experience with other placements, he'll adapt to his new surroundings within a few days. He'll still be a little downhearted every now and then, but I believe, given everything I've learned about you, that you would understand what he's feeling probably better than anyone else."

Ethan's jaw flexed involuntarily. She had no idea.

"The previous couple who wanted to adopt Jerry didn't understand how to handle his disconnect with the family unit. Children who have been through that type of emotional trauma need extra care to build trust. We tried to convey that prior to them taking Jerry into their home, and they had felt certain that it would be a good situation, but—" her mouth curved down at the corners "—it was more difficult than they expected."

Ethan didn't think much more of the couple who'd turned the boy away than he did Jerry's biological parents. But now wasn't the time to judge. Now was the time to let Jerry know that all adults wouldn't necessarily disappoint him. Or hurt him. "I understand what he needs. Someone who will love him unconditionally. Someone who will actually care."

Rose and Daisy attempted to get Jerry to join them on the other side of the fountain. "Come over here." Rose crooked a small finger. "Watch the way they follow the bread into the water. It's so funny."

Jerry took a timid step toward the girls, then tilted his head toward their parents, standing a few feet away, and froze.

"It's okay, Jerry." Brodie took his wife's hand and led her away from the twins toward a wrought iron bench on the opposite side of the fountain. "You can play with Rose and Daisy. We'll sit here and watch you feed the birds."

Savvy shoved her shoulder into the side of his arm. "Geese, Brodie. They're geese." She laughed, and the girls joined in, their happy giggles filling the air.

Jerry blinked several times, watching the joy between the family, and then furrowed his brow. He squeezed his hand so hard around the top of the bag that his tiny knuckles turned white, then he dropped his head and dragged one shoe across the soft earth.

Ethan's heart clenched in pain for the boy. And apparently the social worker's did, too, because she whispered, "God, please help him."

From the night he'd heard Jerry's story on the news, Ethan had wanted the little boy. He knew what Jerry had gone through, and he knew what the child needed. Love. Time. Patience. Protection. Things that had never been given to Jerry before.

And things that had never been given to Ethan.

"Mr. Ethan, we're out of bread." Daisy darted toward the bench, and Rose followed.

He had one more sack. "I have another bag that y'all can share."

Rose's lower lip puckered. "But Jerry is out of bread, too, and that won't be very much for all three of us."

"Rose, don't be greedy," Brodie called from the other side of the fountain. "Say thank you."

"I have two bags."

Ethan didn't recognize the soft, feminine voice, and when he turned to see who'd spoken, he was taken aback by the stunning woman walking toward the group.

She moved shyly and slowly, yet gracefully. She wore a white lace-trimmed blouse topped with a sheer pale pink cardigan and a long floral skirt that nearly reached her white sandals. Strawberry blond hair caught the afternoon sunlight and tumbled freely in red-gold waves past her shoulders.

Ethan waited to see if anyone would introduce the lady, but they all seemed as surprised by her appearance as he was.

"I have some bread that they can have," she repeated. "If that's okay."

As she grew closer, Ethan noticed more details about the striking woman. Arched brows above thick lashes that surrounded vivid blue eyes. Sleek nose, high cheekbones, full lips. And a trickle of endearing pale copper freckles dotting the top of each cheek.

She had one of those faces you would see on a fashion magazine and know that a masterful hand had utilized an abundance of airbrush skills. But this woman hadn't been airbrushed.

In fact, other than a soft sheen of pink gloss on her lips, she didn't appear to wear any makeup at all.

Honestly, he wouldn't have thought anything could take his mind off his potential adoption, and he rarely paid attention to any woman after how badly he'd been burned in the past. But then again, he was a healthy, single, thirty-year-old man, and he appreciated a pretty woman when he saw one.

Pretty?

No.

Beautiful. *Very* beautiful.

And from the way she glanced away when their eyes met, she had no idea.

Lindy's heart lodged in her throat, her skin bristled and, for a moment, she feared she'd go into shock in front of all the adults who seemed way too close. Too close to Lindy.

Too close to her son.

Jerry. He'd grown so much, but she felt certain those were the eyes she'd loved, the cheeks she'd kissed, the little mouth that curved up at the edges when she'd tickled him and he released those precious baby belly giggles that she'd adored.

He wasn't smiling now. His eyes weren't full of life. And he was no longer a baby.

Moreover, he looked…as lost as she felt.

Jerry.

Was this her son? And if he was, how would she ever explain why she'd been gone so long? How did you tell a four-year-old that his mommy never wanted to leave him? How would a four-year-old understand the difference in guilty… and innocent? How could he comprehend that, though a jury had been convinced she was a murderer, they had been so very terribly wrong?

A blond-haired girl with *Daisy* on her shirt ran toward Lindy. "Can I have one of your bags? Rose got the last one from Mr. Ethan." She pointed to the man seated on the park bench nearest Lindy.

Even sitting down, he gave the appearance of tall, dark and—without a doubt—handsome. The kind of handsome that would make most women do a double take. Or simply stare. Lindy jerked her attention away from the man and back to the boy.

"That's Mr. Ethan," Daisy continued. "What's your name?"

Reluctantly, she pulled her gaze from the little boy to the girl. "Lindy," she managed, then, still getting accustomed to using her maiden name again, she added, "Lindy Burnett."

"I like that name." Daisy bobbed her head for emphasis and sent blond pigtails swinging.

"Thank you." Lindy liked the name, too, much more than Melinda Sue Flinn, which would undoubtedly spark recognition. And, most likely, disdain.

"So, can I have one of your bags?" Daisy asked.

"Sure." Lindy handed her the brown sack and then asked the little boy that she believed to be her son, "Do you need some more, too?"

He looked at her, his head tilting for a moment, then his attention turned to the adults gathered around the fountain. And he held his ground.

"He's a little shy." The guy on the nearest bench glanced toward Jerry. "Maybe you can put the bag on the edge by the fountain?"

Her chin wobbled and she felt instantly stung, but she reeled her emotions in and placed the bag where he'd indicated. Then she moved to a vacant park bench to watch the boy she'd dreamed of holding each and every day since he'd been taken from her arms.

Take the bag, sweetie. Come on, please.

She knew she couldn't let this group know who she was, because they were certainly affiliated with the children's home that currently had custody of Jerry. But she needed to connect with her son. Some way. Somehow.

And she had to get him back.

Jerry studied the bag from where he stood, but when an excited black goose with a bright red beak waddled toward it, he quickly put his small feet into action. When he reached the sack, Lindy leaned forward so that she was merely a few feet from the boy.

"Hey there." She studied those clear blue eyes, remembered the first time they'd looked at her, when the nurse had held him close to her face in the delivery room and she'd felt a love like she'd never known before. A connection. A bond that couldn't be separated by space, or time…or prison walls. "What's your name?" She *knew* this was her little man, but she wanted to hear him say it, needed to verify what her heart had already confirmed.

He took the bag, held it for a moment as he looked at her, and then returned to the other side of the fountain to toss his bread.

What had happened to him since she'd been away?

Dear God, please. I need to know. Is he mine? Is that my Jerry?

Her features tight with emotion, she turned toward the man—Ethan—sitting on the adjacent bench and for the first time noticed the woman at the other end. It was easy to understand why she hadn't noticed her before, with the way he captured attention. But Lindy didn't want to notice the dark, wavy hair, the warm brown eyes that looked so kind, so appealing. Or the smile that seemed so sincere. She'd fallen prey to that kind of deception in the past and she wasn't about to make the same mistake again.

So she focused on the woman. She looked to be mid-thirties, with pale blond hair, and was dressed in a crisp white blouse and navy slacks. She seemed intent on surveying the little boy now timidly tossing bread to the geese. She was, no doubt, the social worker assigned to the case.

That explained why she was here, but how did Ethan fit into Jerry's world? And what about the couple with the two girls? Were they the ones she'd heard about, the "good home" that her son would have when the adoption went through?

Lindy could have asked several questions to try to put the pieces together, but instead she asked the one she most needed to know. "Is he okay?"

Ethan released an audible breath, his full lower lip rolling in before he answered, "He will be." His head moved slowly up and down, affirming his resolve. He sounded *so* certain, *so* determined, that Lindy wondered how he could be that sure. Because she didn't see any way Jerry would be okay without his mother.

And she would *never* be okay without her son.

The social worker glanced at her bag, then added, "He's recently been placed at Willow's Haven, the children's home nearby, and he's still adjusting to the new environment. His name is Jerry."

Jerry. Adrenaline burned through her at the mere mention of his name. She'd found him. This *was* her little boy. Her son. Right here. Merely feet away after so many minutes, hours and days—three long years—staring at the walls of a four-by-eight cell and dreaming of seeing him again, longing to hold him again. But the odds were against her, and she had to maintain her composure to have any chance of spending time with him now.

The attorney's words from this morning's conversation echoed through her thoughts.

Your son's adoption may have already been finalized, and if that's the case, it'll be even more difficult for you to obtain custody again through a reverse adoption, where the court basically reverses the decision and returns the child to his biological parent.

Lindy swallowed thickly, looked toward her little boy and silently prayed. *Please, God, You know how much I need him in my life. And You know how much he needs me.* "So is he— Can he be adopted?"

The woman placed a hand on her bulging red satchel. "That's our goal. I'm Candace Yost, the social worker assigned to Jerry's case. Yes, eventually he can be adopted. And I feel certain he'll have his forever home this time." She looked fondly toward Ethan.

A shiver of fear inched down Lindy's spine as the man between Lindy and the social worker—and between Lindy and her son—turned toward her and displayed a smile that typically melted a female's heart, the kind that had once melted Lindy's.

Not anymore. The only male she cared about now was the four-year-old on the other side of the fountain.

"I'm Ethan Green," he said, "and I want to adopt Jerry."

She looked beyond this Ethan Green, who with a simple introduction had become her biggest adversary, and instead focused on Jerry, now feeding the geese. "I do, too."

Lindy's jolt at realizing her little boy was merely feet away had affected her ability to choose words wisely. She'd spoken the truth. She wanted to adopt Jerry. More precisely, she wanted to regain custody of her son. Thankfully, she hadn't made *that* statement, or the looks of surprise on both their faces would more likely have been looks of horror.

"You…want to adopt Jerry?" Ethan's question smacked Lindy with the same rousing force as the water from the fountain hit those determined geese. It woke her up and made her realize her error—and also caused her to look at the man who reminded her of the husband who'd hurt her so badly. The man who intended to adopt her child.

Her. Child.

She needed to rectify her mistake, or she might not get a chance to spend more time with Jerry and find a way to have him in her life again.

"I meant that I would *also* like to adopt a child." She prayed they couldn't hear the wobble in her voice brought on by this landslide of emotions. After quickly organizing her thoughts, she explained, "I—wouldn't be able to adopt right now, though."

The truth of *that* statement slammed her with the same intensity as Nika's fists in the prison yard, when Lindy had mistakenly crossed paths with the inmate known as the Agitator. Or Gil's fists on practically every night of their marriage.

Lindy pushed the horrid memories away and

watched her son, so quiet and withdrawn, the way he'd always been when Gil was at home and he was afraid of his daddy's temper. Even at just fourteen months, he'd known to be fearful of his father. But when it'd just been the two of them in the house, when he'd been alone with Lindy, he'd laughed, smiled, played.

Would he now be consumed by sadness forever?

She wanted to hold him, hug him. But he hadn't recognized her, hadn't known his mother at all.

And why should he? Not only did she look different now, but he'd been a baby when she left. Now he was a little boy. The three years apart might as well have been ten.

He didn't know her.

The social worker cleared her throat. "Why wouldn't you be able to adopt, Lindy?" Her tone was gentle, as though she knew the agony tormenting Lindy's soul.

Lindy wanted to sprint the few feet to Jerry, pick him up and run. She wanted to go somewhere where she could take the time to show him that she loved him, and that she'd never, ever stopped loving him. But that would only make things worse. She needed to find a better way. A right way. A legal way.

Swallowing, she explained, "I couldn't adopt

a child now because I've…had a tough time over the past few years. I don't have a family, or a job, or even a place to live." Her stomach pitched at the truth. "I don't have anything to offer a child."

The couple on the other side of the fountain had started walking toward them and must have overheard her statement, because the woman moved toward Lindy's bench and sat down. "That can't be true," she said softly. "Because the main thing kids need in their lives is love."

Throughout her years at the prison, Lindy had taught herself not to cry. Crying was a weakness, and she couldn't let the other inmates see her as the weakest. Consequently, she'd believed she no longer possessed the ability to release her tears. But they slipped free now, thick, wet drops edging down her cheeks.

Lindy wiped them away. "I don't know what has me so upset." The lie stung. She knew *exactly* what had her upset. Her son was here, right in front of her, and she had no idea what to do to get him back.

Forgive me, Lord. And help me now. Show me how to have Jerry in my life again. She was still trying to work her way back toward trusting God. Though she'd learned in the prison ministry that He'd never leave her, she still wondered where He had been the night the police had torn Jerry from her arms and charged her with her husband's murder.

"Here." Ethan moved toward her, a white handkerchief extended from his hand.

To ignore the offering might make the others wonder what she had against the man, so she took the soft white fabric and swiped at her cheeks. A crisp scent, earthy and masculine, filled her senses. She fought against inhaling deeper. She didn't want to like this man, or the way he smelled, or the fact that, unlike any man she'd ever known, he still carried a handkerchief. "Thank you."

The woman next to her, who now had an arm draped around Lindy's shoulders, echoed her thoughts. "You carry a handkerchief?"

Ethan smiled. "I teach eighth graders. You know, the age when every girl gets her feelings hurt by another girl at some point in the school year. It never hurts to have a handkerchief handy."

He taught school. And seemed nice. How would Lindy ever convince a court that she should have Jerry instead of this man?

Because she knew from past experience how a man could sway her opinion with his gorgeous good looks, or his swoonworthy charm. Gil had fooled the public—and Lindy—into believing he was a great catch and a good guy…

and then had been the exact opposite behind closed doors.

"Here." She attempted to return the handkerchief, but Ethan shook his head.

"You keep it. Like I said, I go through them rather quickly, and I have plenty more." Another charming smile, showing off straight white teeth amid a tan face, threatened to knock her senses off balance. "Seriously, keep it," he said.

Lindy didn't have the wherewithal to argue, so she nodded. "Thanks." Then she caught sight of Jerry, easing toward the fountain with the last bits of his bread.

"Look at that one with the bread on his back," one of the twins said, giggling and pointing.

Jerry followed the direction of her finger and nodded. Lindy felt a sliver of hope. He was interacting with other children and, for a moment, didn't look quite so sad.

She so wanted to see him smile.

"You said you need a job and a place to stay, right?" the lady beside her asked.

"Yes." She'd stayed in cheap—very cheap—hotels over the past week, but after buying the little used car that she'd needed to get to Claremont and purchasing a limited supply of clothing, she'd depleted almost all of the money she'd saved when she'd been married to Gil. Lindy was glad she'd been trying to save for a vehicle back then, or she wouldn't have had anything beyond the ten dollars of "gate money" she'd been given when she was released.

"Well, I happen to know that my grandparents are looking for help at their sporting goods store." She pointed behind Lindy. "I'm Savvy Evans, but my maiden name is Bowers, and my grandparents' store is over there. Bowers's Sporting Goods. I actually worked there before we started the children's home, and let me tell you, you won't find any better people to work for."

"Of course, she's a little prejudiced, but it's the truth." The man beside her grinned. "I'm Savvy's husband, Brodie Evans."

Lindy couldn't believe this turn of events. "You think they might hire me?" She'd already considered the difficulty of finding employment. If there were any sort of application process, or even a request for references, she didn't have a prayer.

Savvy nodded assuredly. "Of course I do."

God, I'm trying to learn to trust You, but how are You going to pull this off?

Savvy continued to smile, and Lindy was struck by how much the offer meant to her. "We were planning to go over there and talk to my grandparents about our new fishing program after we leave the fountain. That's what this position would involve, primarily working with the new Fishers of Men program that we're starting for the kids at Willow's Haven. Why don't you come with us and talk to them about the job?"

Lindy couldn't remember the last time anyone had offered to help her, if ever. Then she thought about the man who'd just given her a handkerchief when she cried. The same one who wanted to adopt her son—and take Jerry away from her permanently.

He looked at her now, and an instant awareness inched through her, the sensation that she'd been noticed by an extremely handsome man. Which was quickly followed by the memory of the last time an attractive man had noticed her. Then married her. And hurt her. Repeatedly.

"Why don't you go with us?" he asked, as though he thought she might want encouragement from him.

She didn't. In fact, she wanted him to leave, to get away from her and, more important, from her son.

"I wanted to go there anyway, to see what Jerry and I will need for the time we're going to spend together this summer. As much as I'll admit I have no clue about fishing, I'm still excited about learning to fish with him." He displayed another smile that punched her in the heart. *He* would be spending time with Jerry this summer.

But so would she.

She turned to Savvy. "I'd like to talk to them about the job."

"Awesome! Let's go." Savvy smiled broadly. So did Ethan.

But Lindy could only pray. Pray that God would give her this chance to be around her little boy on a regular basis. She needed to get to know him again and show him that she loved him while the attorney figured out the best way for her to regain custody.

And if that meant spending time with Ethan Green, so be it.

Chapter Two

Ethan walked with the group toward the sporting goods store and considered how he'd arrived in Claremont this morning with one goal: to begin the process of adopting Jerry and showing this little guy that someone would care about him, someone would love him unconditionally, never abandon him and take care of his every need.

In other words, he wanted to be the kind of father that he'd never had, to a boy who was so much like himself.

Because of Ethan's own past, he'd always been drawn to those who'd been hurt or mistreated. *That* was why he couldn't stop thinking about the woman who'd pierced his heart with her story.

She wanted to adopt a child but didn't think

she had anything to offer. She had no family. No job. No home.

What had happened to Lindy Burnett?

And how could Ethan help?

They reached the sporting goods store, and the twins darted inside to see their great-grandparents, Brodie and Savvy following. But Jerry didn't join the group. Instead, he peered at the window display, which featured a bright green pedal boat suspended in the air and fishing gear propped on a sea of blue fabric.

Candace, Ethan and Lindy stopped near the boy as he placed his palms against the window and examined the items.

"What do you think of all that?" Ethan asked. "Pretty cool, huh?"

Jerry's small fingers curled in as he moved his hands together to bracket his eyes and catch a better view. "Yes," he said, then he jerked his head toward Ethan and quickly added, "sir."

While Ethan was glad Jerry had finally spoken to him, he still glanced to the social worker and wondered if she was thinking the same thing—that the little boy had apparently gotten in trouble in the past for not addressing adults with respect.

What kind of trouble? Ethan wondered. And at whose hand? Who had caused the fear in those bright blue eyes? The last family he'd lived with had wanted to adopt him then decided against it, but Jerry had been in several short-term placements before he'd ended up with them. Undoubtedly, at least one of those homes had put this fear in the boy, because Jerry would've been too young to have worried about saying "sir" to Gil Flinn.

How many people had already hurt this child?

Lindy's mouth turned down at the edges, and then she slowly crouched next to Jerry at the window, her long floral skirt gathering around her as she spoke to the doleful boy. "That green thing is called a pedal boat," she said softly. "I always thought it would be fun to try one, but I've never had the chance." She pulled at the edges of her pink cardigan as she leaned against the brick building and looked directly into Jerry's eyes. Ethan was thrown once again by the sheer beauty of the woman, particularly as she spoke so tenderly to the boy. "Do you think it'd be fun, Jerry?" she asked.

"Yes, ma'am." He nodded, but then shook his head. "No." He paused. "No, ma'am."

Lindy's lower lip trembled, and Ethan stepped closer.

"You don't think that'd be fun, Jerry?" he asked.

Another emphatic shake, and Ethan wondered what had just transpired in the boy's head. Why had he changed his mind so quickly? More fear?

Lindy released a heavy breath that reflected Ethan's feelings. She looked pained, as if she felt as much agony over the child's situation as Ethan.

Did she?

"Why don't we go in the store, Jerry, and see what else they have, okay?" Candace prompted, placing a palm against Jerry's back to guide him away from the window.

Ethan stepped ahead to open the door for his future son. "Want to head inside, Jerry?"

Still staring at the pedal boat, he shook his head, as though answering a silent question, then he eased away from the window and entered the store. Candace followed, while Ethan held the door.

But Lindy remained crouched near the window. Her petite features were drawn, and a heavy tear slid down her left cheek. She made no effort to wipe it away, and Ethan watched as it moved past her jaw and then trickled down the slender column of her throat.

I don't have a family, or a job, or even a place to live.

Like Jerry, the attractive woman's world had been upended.

But how?

She slowly stood and discreetly brushed the side of her hand along the path the tear had taken. "He wants to be strong, but he's scared."

Ethan thought the same thing, because he knew from experience. But how was she so sure? What had happened in *her* world? He released his hold on the door and allowed it to close, not wanting Jerry to overhear his words. "I have to wonder how I—or how any adult—will ever gain his trust."

She chewed her lower lip and then swallowed. "It'll take time, but I have to show him he can trust again."

"*You* have to show him?" Ethan asked. Why would she think that was her responsibility?

"We," she corrected herself. "We—adults—have to show him that he can trust again."

The door opened, and Savvy peeked out. "Hey, my grandparents are eager to meet y'all."

Daisy stuck her head out near Savvy's hip and peered up at her. "Mom, come look at the new pink and purple life jackets they've got." She tugged on the hem of Savvy's shirt. "They're girl colors, and one even has flowers on it."

Savvy grinned. "I should go check those out." She looked at Lindy and raised a finger. "Something to note, sporting goods stores aren't just for guys anymore." Then she smiled, and left them alone again.

"You may want to bring that up when you're interviewing for the job," he said, trying to lighten things and put her more at ease before she talked to the owners.

Lindy blinked, her long lashes still damp as she nodded. "Thanks, I will."

Ethan suddenly recalled the last time he'd wanted to help a beautiful, troubled female. He'd only meant to give Jenny comfort and be a friend to her after she'd lost her parents. But he'd ended up falling for his friend. They'd grown closer, and both proclaimed love. Planned to be together forever. Gotten engaged. And then he'd lost his fiancée *and* his best man, when she'd left Ethan for Sean.

No doubt Lindy Burnett needed someone to care about her, someone to help her, maybe even someone to love her. But Ethan could only go so far. He could be kind. He could attempt to help. But he couldn't let himself fall in love.

He could also pray for her and ask God to give her the job she needed, the child she wanted, the life she desired. That was what he could do, what he should do.

What he would do.

And he'd maintain the reins on his heart, the way he'd vowed to do after Jenny had left him two days before their wedding and married Sean six months later.

He opened the door again. "Ready to go get that job?"

She stepped through the entrance, Ethan trying not to notice the way her freckles looked more copper up close, or how her strawberry waves swayed against her shoulder when she moved, or that she smelled like sweet honey.

God, help her get this job. Help her adopt a child. Help her have a family again. Help her find love. And, God, help me keep my mind on Jerry...and off her.

He entered and turned away from Lindy, who was already speaking to Savvy about the potential job, and looked for the boy who would hopefully be his son soon.

Ethan perused the immaculate store, impressed with the amount of inventory. The floor space wasn't large, yet Savvy's grandparents had organization down to an art, with each section identified by sport. Football, basketball, soccer and baseball composed the front left side. Supplies for outdoor activities, such as kayaks, tents and fishing gear, filled the front right. The back of the store held items for golfing, tennis, track and so on.

"Look at this, Jerry. What do you think?" He selected a tiny leather T-ball glove from one of the wire baskets hanging along the left wall. Growing up, Ethan had enjoyed baseball. In Alabama, they kept the sport going year-round, which had worked for him, since he was always moving from one foster home to another. He didn't have to learn a new activity, and by high school, he was known for having a pretty good arm. Pretty good swing, too, truth be told.

"Want to try it on? I can show you how it fits over your hand, and maybe we could go to a field around here and learn to catch some baseballs." Ethan's blood pumped fiercely, excitement palpable as he imagined this summer and all the days he and Jerry would spend at the local park. "Doesn't that sound great?"

The little boy looked glumly at the glove and said nothing.

Candace knelt beside him and offered him a smile. "Jerry, would you like to play baseball sometime with Mr. Green? You can tell us if you don't want to, or you can tell us if you do."

Ethan could almost see himself in the scene before him, a tiny little boy listening to his social worker trying to sort out what was going on in his mind. They'd all been so nice, but he'd never had the courage to tell them the truth. What did he want? A real home. To stop moving every year. Or every month. He'd wanted a dad who loved him and cared for him. And a mom who wouldn't stand by while his father beat him until, at merely six years old, Ethan could no longer stand.

"I don't want to play baseball." Jerry's soft words weren't delivered to Candace, but to Ethan.

He didn't want to play baseball. That ruined Ethan's vision, but still…he'd answered Ethan. Not Candace, but Ethan.

"Okay, then, we'll do something else," he said, regrouping his plans for father/son time. No baseball, no problem. He already knew they would be fishing together, since the Fishers of Men program was planned for every child at Willow's Haven. Ethan had hoped, though, that they might find something in common that he had some sort of experience with. But in any case, he indicated the fishing items on the opposite side of the store. "We can go look at the fishing gear with Rose and Daisy if you want."

Jerry didn't answer, but he nodded. Another step in the right direction.

Ethan and Candace led him toward Brodie and the girls, who were checking out kid-sized fishing rods displayed in a bright yellow bucket. Savvy had taken Lindy to the back of the store to talk to her grandparents about the potential job. He watched as Savvy made introductions, and Lindy's hand moved back to her throat as she gave them a watery smile.

How could someone so stunning have so little confidence?

"We're excited about the Fishers of Men program," Brodie said. "We weren't sure we'd be able to get enough mentors from the community, but one announcement at church and a few flyers placed at the businesses around the square led to plenty."

Ethan turned his attention from Lindy's interview to Brodie. "Yeah, it seems like a great way for folks to spend time with the kids." And Jerry was looking at the fishing gear with interest, which was better than the baseball glove fail.

Brodie examined the white price tag on a fishing rod. "Learning to fish and enjoying God's creation—a terrific way to bond with the kids. It was Savvy's idea, of course." He picked up the rod, weighed it in his hand and grinned. "She's always coming up with ways to involve the community in the kids' lives."

"Sounds like so much fun," Candace said, tilting her head toward Jerry and pulling a red fishing rod from the yellow bucket.

Ethan didn't know the first thing about fishing. Nothing. He'd never had anyone take him to a lake or teach him to put one of those reels on the rod or even show him how to bait a hook.

But Jerry, holding the red fishing rod, looked at him now as though waiting for someone to offer to do something with him…the same way Ethan had always prayed for someone to spend time with him.

Seriously, God? Peter, Andrew, James and John were fishermen. But me? I haven't got a clue. You know that. Why not baseball?

Yet Ethan found himself asking, "You want to be my fishing buddy for the summer, Jerry?"

Jerry looked at the rod, and then at Ethan. "Yes, sir."

No, it wasn't his sport of choice, but Jerry actually wanted to fish…with Ethan. Ethan wanted to pick the kid up, swing him around and cheer, but they weren't anywhere near that point. Yet. Instead, he took a deep breath and prayed that he wouldn't stink too badly at fishing. *Okay, Lord. Here we go.* "Well, all right, then."

Candace smiled. "A perfect opportunity to bond, don't you think?"

"I do." Ethan couldn't disagree, even if he wondered how many other adults would be watching him. He'd have to pray no one caught the process on video. He could just imagine his students having a field day with Mr. Green's botched fishing experience.

"Some of my best memories growing up are from fishing with my friends." Brodie grinned. "I remember one time John Cutter hooked my ear on a cast that went wrong." He touched his right ear. "Still got the scar from that one."

Ethan winced and instinctively cupped a hand over one ear. "I hope we don't make those kind of memories, Jerry, don't you?"

Jerry squinted up at him, and gave him something that resembled a grin.

Ethan's pulse tripped, and his heart soared. Fishing. If that was what it took to make Jerry happy and able to trust him, then that's what Ethan would do. "So I guess I'll need to start purchasing some of this fishing gear?"

"You can, or you can just rent the equipment for the summer, whatever works best. Savvy's grandparents do provide a fifty percent discount to folks participating in the program, so if you think you may want to keep fishing after it's done, that'd be a great deal."

Ethan didn't want Jerry seeing anything they did together as short-term, so he quickly answered, "That's what we'll want."

"I thought you might." Brodie leaned down to help Rose and Daisy, who'd managed to get two fishing rods locked together. "Savvy's grandparents have a list of recommended supplies. Why don't you go get a copy and find out when all of the gear we've requested for the program will be available in the store? They were supposed to hear from the supplier this morning."

"Sounds good." Ethan left the group and worked his way through circular racks of life jackets and hip waders to find Savvy and an older gentleman filling a square purple bin with small tackle boxes.

"These will be great for the kids," she said, then noticed him approaching. "Hey, Ethan, this is my grandfather, James Bowers. Granddaddy, this is Ethan Green. He's the man I told y'all about, the one who wants to adopt the little boy who came to Willow's Haven a few days ago."

"That's wonderful, son." Mr. Bowers extended a hand. "Pleasure to meet you."

"Nice to meet you." Ethan could get used to the friendliness of this town. Birmingham was a friendly place, too, but with a population of 200,000 compared to Claremont's roughly 4,500, it lacked the everyone-knows-everyone feeling of Claremont. And Ethan found that he liked it, a lot.

"Everything going okay up front with the kids?" Savvy asked.

"Yes, but I wanted to see about getting a list of supplies for the Fishers of Men program." He spotted a small blue lifejacket and thought it'd probably be Jerry's size. He'd need to add that to the list. They wouldn't need it for fishing on the bank, but if they ventured out on a boat, he'd need one. He thought about the pedal boat and Jerry's apparent fear. And the fact that Lindy had picked up on it, too.

Maybe she had that kind of intuition—a mother's intuition.

But she didn't have children. She'd said she had no family.

"Ah, right. The list for the Fishers of Men program," Mr. Bowers said. "The printouts are in the office. Ask Jolaine to give you a copy. She's in there talking to our newest employee." He grinned, and Ethan did, too. Lindy had apparently gotten the job she needed.

"The office is back there, far right corner," Savvy said, gesturing with her thumb over her shoulder.

"Thanks." Ethan headed for the office, but slowed when he got close and heard Savvy's grandmother and Lindy talking.

Lindy already adored the woman sitting across from her. Jolaine Bowers reminded her of her own grandmother, the one who'd raised

Lindy and shown her the true meaning of unconditional love.

"So like I was saying, I had just said amen after asking God to get us some help for the summer, and then you came walking in," Jolaine said.

The way she looked at Lindy now, her blue eyes radiating compassion, proved she wasn't questioning whether Lindy would be a good employee or judging her or wondering about her background. "Isn't that something, the way God works?"

Lindy wanted to simply agree and be done with it, take the job and spend her summer with Jerry until she got her son back for good, but that seemed way too easy. "Mrs. Bowers, I appreciate this opportunity. And I really need and want the job, but I have to be honest. You haven't said anything about me filling out an application, and you should know that I don't have any experience. In fact—" her voice hitched "—there are no real reasons you should hire me."

Savvy's grandmother leaned forward in her weathered brown desk chair, watching Lindy with undeniable kindness, as if she were sitting with her own granddaughter. "Honey, which part of me praying for you, and then you walking in didn't you understand?" She placed her hand on top of Lindy's as she spoke, and the warmth of it radiated up Lindy's arm and straight to her heart.

"Mrs. Bowers, I can't tell you how much your trust in me means, especially since you just met me." Truthfully, Lindy couldn't understand why the couple would have that kind of faith in a woman they didn't know.

"Sweetie, my trust is in God, and He hasn't steered me wrong. He sent you here today, I'm certain of it." She gave Lindy an exaggerated wink.

In spite of what Lindy had learned about God from the prison ministry, she still wasn't certain how much He could actually do. Or how He could keep her past from crippling her future. And her past would come out, along with the fact that, even though she was innocent of murder, she hadn't protected her child. But regarding this position, she had no one to vouch that she'd be a good employee. Her grandmother had passed away six months after Lindy had been convicted. "I don't have any references."

"God sent you. That's the only reference I need. And from what Savvy said, you don't have a place to stay in Claremont yet. Is that right?"

Not only did she not have a place to stay, she

didn't have much of anything else either. She'd need more clothes for sure, but she'd seen a cute little consignment shop on the other side of the square that might have decent clothes at a price she could manage. "I don't have a place to stay," she admitted.

"Well, then, I meant to tell you that part of this job includes staying on-site, in case we have any after-hours deliveries and things like that. We have a little apartment upstairs where you can live, so that you'll be here to help us out for those kinds of things."

Lindy couldn't help but ask, "Mrs. Bowers, was that a part of the job before you knew I needed a place to stay?"

"Now, sweetie, I know you're not trying to talk me into fibbing," she said, tilting her head in a "don't go there" gesture that melted Lindy. "It's a part of the job now, and that's what matters. And the place isn't anything fancy, but it'll do."

Lindy swallowed thickly, nodded and felt another batch of tears coming. She'd gone three years without a single droplet, and now the floodgates had opened.

The woman pointed a finger at Lindy. "Hey, now, we don't allow tears in here. That's cause for firing, you know." Then she laughed, which sounded more like a teenager's giggle than a grandmother's. "Just kidding. Let me find you a tissue."

"It's okay. I have this." Lindy held up Ethan's handkerchief, wiped at her face and again smelled that crisp masculine scent that reminded her of the man who seemed so perfect. She finished dabbing at her face and put the handkerchief away. "I'll be fine. I just haven't had anyone be this nice to me in…a while." Except for the heart-stoppingly handsome man who had given her the handkerchief…and who wanted her son.

"Well, then, we both had prayers answered today, I'd say." Mrs. Bowers peeked around Lindy. "Oh, hello. You must be Ethan. Savvy told us about you, and how you're planning to adopt that precious little boy."

Lindy turned, surprised to find him behind her and wondering how much he'd heard. She hated the way her heart tripped over itself at the sight of the good-looking man, the same way it had fluttered the first time she'd seen Gil Flynn. When would she ever learn? She was in no place to think about romance. In fact, the only thing she should be thinking about—focusing on with every fiber of her being, rather—was her son.

Ethan cleared his throat, one corner of his mouth lifting as though he knew how his mere appearance affected her heart rate. "I apologize for interrupting, but Mr. Bowers said you would have the supply list for the Fishers of Men program, and it looks like I'm going to need to purchase some fishing equipment for me and Jerry."

"Is that so?" Mrs. Bowers clasped her hands together. "Well, isn't that nice?" She shifted toward the desk and moved stacks of papers and files and sports magazines aside. "You know that you do have the option to rent the equipment, if you'd rather not have that kind of investment in it."

"Brodie told me, but to tell you the truth, I don't want Jerry to see anything I do with him as temporary. I want him to know I'm here to stay." The other side of his mouth joined in for a full, pulse-skittering grin.

But Lindy was nowhere near smiling in return, especially after hearing he planned on a long-term commitment…with *her* son.

Mrs. Bowers, however, grinned broadly. "That's so wonderful!" She withdrew a sheet of paper from a manila folder and handed it to Ethan. "Here you go then. We've got a bunch of kids signed up from Willow's Haven, and the church is still matching them with mentors, but we should have all of our supplies in the store and ready to get started by Monday."

She handed the file to Lindy. "You'll be the main one running the program, so I might as well give you this."

Lindy accepted the folder, opened it and glanced down at the list of supplies, which included a fishing schedule at the bottom of the page.

"So we fish twice a week?" Ethan must have noticed the same thing.

"You do. Either Monday and Wednesday, or Tuesday and Thursday. You're welcome to come on Fridays and Saturdays, too, if you want, but we don't open on Sunday. That day is for the Lord," Mrs. Bowers said, then turned her attention back to Lindy. "And you'll be helping them with supplies, manning the store at the fishing hole while they're all fishing, that type of thing. It isn't a difficult job, but you'll be busy."

"I see that," she said, still scanning the schedule, "but that's okay. I like being busy, and I sure need the work."

Mrs. Bowers gave her another wink and clicked her tongue against the roof of her mouth. "You're gonna be a pro at this, I can tell."

"I hope so," Lindy said, praying that she would also be a pro at interacting with her son and proving that she deserved him in her life again.

Mrs. Bowers tapped the paper. "They have forty-eight kids at Willow's Haven. We've divided them into two groups, so you'll have twenty-four who come Monday and Wednesday with their mentors, and then the others come Tuesday and Thursday. And like I told Ethan, they all have the option of fishing on the weekends, too, if they want. That may be more work hours than you had intended."

"It's fine," Lindy said. More than fine, because she'd be showing the court that she could earn an income while also getting more time with Jerry. "In fact, it's perfect."

"Wonderful!" Mrs. Bowers clasped her fingers beneath her chin as though Lindy really had been the answer to her prayers.

And maybe she had.

Lindy leaned forward and hugged the lady. "Thank you, Mrs. Bowers. This—this is perfect."

"No. Thank *you*, dear."

Ethan cleared his throat. "Well, since I'm going to be mentoring Jerry, I guess we'll be seeing each other on a regular basis, too."

Lindy's stomach roiled. "I guess we will."

Chapter Three

Lindy unpacked an assortment of fishing tackle on Monday morning, her skin bristling with nerves about the day ahead. Surely she'd interact with Jerry, and hopefully she'd hear from the attorney about starting the process of getting her son back in her life. The two things she'd yearned for—prayed for—throughout the weekend.

But she'd also see Ethan Green. And she certainly hadn't yearned for that. He was too appealing and way too charming. The kind of guy a court would believe had Jerry's best interests at heart and could supply his every need.

And the kind of guy who might be a bad parent behind closed doors, the way Gil had been.

"Would you mind putting a bunch of those colorful sponge fish in the new display out front? I want the Willow's Haven children to see some of their choices in the window before they enter the store." Mrs. Bowers smiled. Lindy realized she did that quite a lot. She hadn't seen a lot of smiles, if any, over the past three years. She attempted one in return, but she feared it came out as timid as she felt.

Thankfully, the woman didn't seem to notice. She pointed toward the checkout counter. "There's a new box over there by the cash register if you want to use those. Sound good?"

"Sure, I'd be happy to." Lindy scooped up the box and carried it to the front, climbed around the curtain separating the display from the store and opened it to view a rainbow of soft sponge fish that the kids would use to practice casting. She withdrew a bright red one and squeezed it between her thumb and forefinger. Jerry had always preferred his red toys as a baby. His red rattle. His red plastic truck. She suspected he'd select at least one red fish for his practice bait.

She placed the squishy fish near the window, then began situating the other colorful sponges in and around the seams of aqua blue tulle that created the "water" in the window. The kids were due to arrive in an hour, and she, as well as Mr. and Mrs. Bowers, had been busy all morning getting everything ready.

So intent on making the area look nice for Jerry and all the other Willow's Haven children, Lindy didn't notice anyone enter the store, or she'd have been marginally prepared for the startlingly handsome man with an equally shocking husky voice who suddenly joined her in the tiny space.

"Can I help?"

Lindy dropped a fistful of fish, so that a clump of the vibrant bait covered one of the seams and looked more like a multicolored loofah than individual fish. But what woman would be able to concentrate—or hang on to those miniature sponges—with Ethan Green this near? He was tall, dark and dangerous. Maybe not dangerous to everyone, but definitely to Lindy, since he planned to adopt her son.

She prayed the new attorney, Ted Murrell, would take her case and that she could get away from—and get Jerry away from—this intimidating man.

"Sorry." His mouth inched into a crooked grin that somehow made him even more appealing. "I didn't mean to scare you. I assumed you heard me enter."

But the goosebumps traveling up her arms had nothing to do with his sudden appearance and everything to do with how the mere presence of the mesmerizing male made her pulse race.

When would she ever learn?

Lindy moistened her lips, gathered her composure and accepted the fact that the man working his way into the display window had no intention of leaving. "No, I didn't hear you. I—had my mind on other things." Like wondering if red was still her little boy's favorite color. And praying that she could somehow get a court to pick her over Ethan.

"I get that way sometimes, lost in my thoughts, usually when I have one of my students on my mind. So many kids growing up in broken homes, you know, and they bring that with them to the classroom." He shrugged and reached for a handful of fish. "Sometimes I'm the only father figure in a kid's life. I know I'm the teacher and not the dad, but it's still a big responsibility, having that kind of impact in a child's world."

Lindy found her hand in the box at the same moment that he reached inside. Their fingers brushed, and she yanked hers out without capturing a single fish.

He noticed, studying her hands, now clenched against her stomach, and then looking at her with confusion…and speculation.

Don't ask why I'm so jittery. Don't. Ask.

Except for the prison guards and, on rare occasions, her state-appointed attorney, she hadn't been around any men over the last three years. And she feared this one more than any other because he was eerily similar to the male who'd fooled her so well—and hurt her so deeply—in the past. Charming. Disarmingly good-looking. And appealing in an "I could be your very best friend and also an absolutely amazing husband" kind of way.

Before he could mention her nervousness, she tried to get the conversation back on track. "It's nice that you're a father figure to those kids." She picked up the discarded fish and placed them sporadically around the fabric. "Is that what made you want to adopt Jerry?"

Of all the kids needing a good home, why had he selected her son?

His eyebrows dipped and his mouth eased to the side as though he wasn't sure he wanted to answer. Had she said too much? Could he tell how badly she wanted to know why he'd picked her kid?

"You don't have to tell me if you don't want to. That was probably too personal of a question for me to ask." She pushed the fabric of her skirt aside to place more of the fish in an empty space, ignoring the way his eyes studied her, making her feel as though he somehow sensed the torment in her soul.

She needed her son in her life, and this magnetic man was her biggest obstacle.

God, please help me.

He took a deep breath, let it out and answered, "I've wanted to adopt Jerry for three years now, ever since I saw his story on the news."

Lindy's pulse accelerated so quickly she could feel her blood pushing in her veins, but she managed to hang onto the sponge fish and quietly asked, "His story on the news?"

"You may have seen it—" he shrugged "—or not. I made a point to watch for it each night after I heard about what happened. He was just over a year old and had been abused. I couldn't stand the thought of a child being hurt, beaten by his father."

"Bless his heart." Though anyone would make the same statement, no one would mean the words as much as Lindy. She hated that Jerry had been hurt, and she'd done her best to stop it.

She just hadn't been strong enough.

"I decided that I wanted to take care of him, to adopt him. I wanted to be the kind of father to him that he never had." He lifted a shoulder. "I missed him this weekend. I just met him, and I missed him already. Hard to believe, huh?"

"Yes." Did she believe him?

"I went back to Birmingham for the weekend," he said.

"So you aren't staying in Claremont?" If he

was driving back and forth from Birmingham, a two-hour drive each way, he'd have less time to spend with Jerry.

"Oh, no, I'm staying here for the summer." He scooted backward to rest against the wall, settling in as though he planned to chat a while. "I just had to go get my things from my house."

Lindy pushed her back teeth together to fight the urge to frown. He *wasn't* driving back and forth each day. And he owned a *house*. A place where Jerry could live that probably had a neighborhood filled with potential friends, a big backyard where he could play and maybe even keep a puppy, and was undoubtedly located in a good school zone.

The kind of place she'd always wanted to live with her son.

She, on the other hand, was staying rent-free in a small room above the sporting goods store. *Free, until you get on your feet*, Mrs. Bowers had said.

How long would that take? And would the court believe she could ever get on her feet? Would *anyone* trust her to take care of her son?

The first attorney she'd contacted after being released had homed in on the fact that would hurt her the most in court. Regardless of whether or not she abused Jerry, she hadn't stopped Gil or reported him to the authorities. Lindy knew she should have, but she also knew that he would have killed her if she did.

Then who would've protected Jerry?

That attorney had turned her case down, but the one from this morning had sounded as though he was considering representing her.

Ethan shifted his large frame against the wall, and Lindy found her attention focusing on his broad shoulders, the hard plates of his chest, visible in spite of his shirt, and biceps that didn't appear to have come from merely lifting papers in a classroom.

More goose bumps traipsed across her skin. She was so easily captivated by this beautiful man.

"I hadn't planned on staying here for the summer," he admitted, while Lindy tried to focus more on his words and less on his appearance. "I actually thought I could pick Jerry up last week, take him home and foster him until the adoption finalized. I went through the ten weeks of fostering certification classes and everything, but then the social worker and the state decided I should spend more time with him first, so he doesn't end up going through another placement that doesn't work out."

She was glad she'd been focusing on his words; she hadn't heard anything about a prior placement for her son. "What do you mean, another placement that doesn't work out?" She knew very little about what had happened to her baby over the past three years, but this hint at Jerry's past didn't sit well with her. What had happened to him?

"The previous family decided they didn't want him." Ethan shook his head. "Gotta tell you, it'd probably be a very good thing if I never meet that couple who'd decided not to keep him."

Lindy's stomach instantly churning, she turned to face him as he tucked more fish in and around the blue water. "Why didn't they want Jerry?" She'd assumed he'd always been in homes like Willow's Haven. Of course, Lindy had only learned bits and pieces about Jerry's location from the state social worker who'd had pity on her after she'd been released from Tutwiler Prison. She'd had to put the woman's cryptic clues together to even find out where the state had placed him. But she'd found him. And now she had to figure out how to get him back in her life permanently.

"Hard to believe, isn't it?" The concern in his tone sounded sincere. "Apparently, he wasn't as social as they'd have liked, and he cried too much." In his left hand was a fish, and Lindy watched as his right one curled into a fist.

Was he like Gil?

"I don't have any sympathy for people like that, turning their backs on a child because of what he's been through, as if he could control his past. Kids need someone they can count on."

Lindy swallowed. "Yes, they do." And Jerry could count on her. He *could.* If only a court would agree.

Ethan leaned a few fish against the corner. "I couldn't wait to get back to Claremont and see Jerry this morning. I think that's why I showed up so early." He grinned. "And to help a lady in need with her window display."

"I don't need anything," Lindy said quickly. Too quickly, from the way his eyebrows inched up and his mouth flattened. She cleared her throat. "I mean, I could've handled it, but I appreciate the help."

A lie. An outright lie. But it was out there, and Ethan didn't look as suspicious, so she let it stand.

Sorry, God. I'm out of my element here, and I'm clearly slipping.

A tap on the window caused both of them to turn toward a little redheaded, freckle-faced boy who was waving, while his mother stood behind him, also waving at the pair in the window. Lindy held up a hand, and Ethan did, as well. Then the two passed by the store and headed toward an old-fashioned barber shop, complete with a red-and-white-striped pole by the entrance.

"Maybe I'll take Jerry there for a haircut one day, since we'll be in Claremont for the summer. That'll be some good father-son bonding, too." He picked up a green fish and held it toward Lindy as he spoke. "I sure hadn't planned on spending the summer fishing. Don't know the first thing about it." He shrugged slightly and gave an easy grin. "But it'll be fun learning with my little man."

His references to her son bothered her immensely, but she did her best to hide the emotion and prayed again that Ted Murrell would take her case, in spite of her inability to pay him anytime in the near future.

A group of children darted across the grass in front of the fountain, and Lindy leaned toward the window. "Is that them?" she whispered anxiously, then felt more anxious being in closer proximity to the man beside her. She cleared her throat and scooted back, glad that he didn't seem to notice.

The cluster of six or seven kids entered the Tiny Tots Treasure Box, the toy store on the opposite side of the square.

Ethan checked his watch. "We still have twenty minutes until eleven, but I'm anxious to see them, too. Really looking forward to spending time with Jerry again."

"I saw him yesterday." She wasn't sure why she divulged the information, but she'd started now, so she'd finish. "At church. I went to church with Mr. and Mrs. Bowers, and all of the Willow's Haven kids came together."

He put the fish against the window and nodded. "Candace mentioned that they all go to Claremont Community Church, and I plan to attend, as well. I couldn't yesterday, of course, since I was in Birmingham. How did he seem? Did you get a chance to talk to him? I thought he started coming out of his shell a little on Friday."

His concern seemed so genuine that Lindy was momentarily taken aback. Did he already care about Jerry? Really care?

But then she remembered the doting-father act that Gil put on in public.

"I didn't get to talk to him." The words hurt, because she'd hoped to communicate with her little boy, but the Willow's Haven children all sat together, and Mr. and Mrs. Bowers had kept her busy meeting all of their friends after the service until the bus filled with children had returned to the home.

"Right. I'm sure there were a lot of people at

the service. Not sure why I thought you would have talked to my little man."

The "my little man" thing hurt, but she didn't want him to think she didn't care about Jerry. "I would have, but I didn't get the chance."

"Well, we'll both see him—and all of the other kids from Willow's Haven—soon, won't we?"

Soon? She'd been counting the minutes. "Yes, we will."

Scanning the display, he asked, "Do you have fishing rods that go with these practice fish? Maybe we could put a few against the sides so the kids can see them."

Lindy had been so wrapped up in thoughts about her son and trying to avoid the effect Ethan Green had on her senses that she nearly forgot why they were sitting in the store window. "We have several boxes in the back. I'll go get one."

He held up a palm. "Let me. You have a lapful of fish." He pointed to her fish-covered skirt and then moved the curtain aside to exit the display area.

Lindy hadn't realized what she'd done, but she'd been so determined not to accidentally touch him again that she'd grabbed an abundance of fish from the box, rather than risk slipping her hand inside…and finding his.

God, I'm struggling here. I need Your help. She thought of her little boy, placed in a home where he wasn't happy and where the parents didn't soothe him when he cried. *And please help Jerry to be okay. And let me help him, Lord. Let me have him in my life again. I need him. I need him so very much.*

"Found them." Ethan entered the display area holding one of the boxes filled with child-sized rods and reels. But with the box of fish already centering the display, there was hardly room for the man and the additional props.

"Maybe I should put them out on my own. It's getting a little crowded." Lindy reached for the box of fish so she could move it toward her, and her hands met the cardboard edge at the same moment as his. But this time, his palms covered hers, and when she jerked her attention to his face, he looked at her as though wondering just how badly she wanted to remove them.

Ethan had been trained to spot children who had been abused. In fact, he'd been required to view an extensive video series on the subject that had made him extremely uncomfortable. However, he *had* been able to spot the signs more clearly after learning what to look for.

But even though his training had been geared

toward abused children, he didn't miss the signs in adults, as well. And he knew without a doubt that Lindy Burnett, at some point in her life, had been abused.

"Lindy, are you okay?" He asked the question as softly as possible, in the same tone he'd use with one of his students, because the beautiful woman across from him, her strawberry hair tumbling forward and those vivid blue eyes filled with an agony that couldn't be disguised, seemed more fragile than any student he'd ever approached with questions of abuse. And Ethan realized that he hadn't merely missed Jerry this weekend; he'd missed this intriguing woman, too.

In fact, he'd be lying if he said he hadn't also shown up early because he knew she'd be here in the store, and that he might have a chance to spend time with her, like this. But there was something troubling the gorgeous lady, and in spite of knowing he shouldn't get too close, Ethan wanted—needed—to help.

She blinked, cleared her throat, and then slowly slid her hands from beneath his. "I'm fine." She made a sound like a combination of a cough and a hiccup, then repeated herself. "I am fine." She looked away to place more fish on the opposite side, or to hide her face so he couldn't see too much, with those long, strawberry tendrils tumbling forward.

He knew he shouldn't be so concerned with this striking lady. Past experience had taught him that the more he cared, the more he'd get hurt when yet another woman in his life let him down. But she seemed so very broken. And Ethan couldn't ignore the need to help someone who'd clearly been abused.

She wasn't fine; he was certain of that. But he was equally certain that she wouldn't discuss it with him. Not yet. Maybe not ever.

And he hadn't come to Claremont to determine what was wrong with this troubled woman. He was here for Jerry. Even so, it was all he could do not to reach forward, push those long strawberry curls out of the way so he could attempt to see what she was trying so desperately to hide.

He swallowed, knowing he shouldn't push. "Okay, then." Picking up a green fishing rod, he grabbed a yellow fish from the box. Determined to think about his future son instead of the enthralling lady beside him, he threaded the fishing line through the tiny hole in the fish's mouth. "Might as well get some of these ready to go." He knotted the line in place. "Maybe Jerry will want this one."

She jerked her head up to answer, tossing

those curls over her shoulder which made her look even more appealing. "He'll want a red one."

Ethan laughed, glad that she hadn't shut herself out of conversation with him completely and also bemused by her statement. What would make her think he'd want red? "You sound so sure of that."

"I..." She paused, her eyes wide, as though she wasn't certain what to say. Then she added, "I think little boys like red."

He shrugged. "Actually, red is my favorite color. Maybe it'll be his, too." He started to reach for the red fishing rod, but then his phone rang in his pocket. Withdrawing the cell, he glanced at the display. "It's Candace, the social worker." He held up a finger. "I'll be right back."

Lindy nodded as Ethan made his way out of the display area. "Hi, Candace. I didn't expect to hear from you today."

"Ethan." He heard her regretful tone.

"Did something happen? Is everything okay with Jerry?"

"Listen, I don't want this to disappoint you, or in any way change your mind about your desire to adopt Jerry, but I have some news. And, well, it really shouldn't affect anything, because I feel certain that the state will uphold the parental rights termination. Terminated means terminated, after all. At least as far as the social workers are concerned."

His chest tightened. She was talking about the little boy he'd missed all weekend, the little boy he wanted so badly that it hurt. "What is it, Candace?"

"It's Jerry's mother, Melinda Sue Flinn. There were some—" she paused "—new developments in her case."

"New developments?" he asked, his mind reeling. How could that be? "She was tried and found guilty of murdering her husband. Her rights were terminated. And I am adopting her son soon. What *kind* of new developments? Tell me the court didn't change the termination of rights."

"No, that didn't change, and I'm totally under the impression that it won't. I have no reservations in saying that she shouldn't ever get her rights back. She didn't protect Jerry, and I will gladly testify to that in court if I need to."

"Then what changed?" Ethan couldn't imagine what would classify as a new development when a wife had been tried by a jury and found guilty of murdering her husband. She'd been sentenced to time in Tutwiler Prison. "Candace, I need to know. What happened?"

"Ethan, her conviction was overturned. She

was released last week. Melinda Sue Flinn is free, and—" she hesitated "—she wants her son back."

Chapter Four

Lindy listened as Ethan's voice lowered, and his shock escalated.

"What do you mean, she's free?" He'd obviously taken a few steps away from the window display, but because he was the sole customer in the store and because Lindy strained her ears to hear, she didn't miss a whispered word. "She was tried and found guilty of murder, Candace. Sentenced to Tutwiler for life. How could the state release her now?"

A cold, bitter frisson shimmied down Lindy's spine at the mere mention of that horrid place, as did a trickle of fear that Ethan could be very close to finding out who she was. Surely the social worker hadn't figured that out.

"A confession? What kind of confession?" He sounded almost as shocked as she had been when she heard the unexpected news, that her best friend had stabbed her in the back to save her own husband, Gil's former business partner. Marsha's testimony about the abuse, as well as how Lindy had confided that she had to get out of the marriage one way or another, had convinced the jury she was guilty. But Marsha had lied. And no one, not even Lindy, had suspected that Paul had murdered the man who had once been his best friend.

Lindy forced her hands to keep moving, situating the fishing rods, placing the fish, anything to control the urge to bolt from the store, find Jerry and take him as far away from Claremont—and Ethan Green—as possible.

But where would they go? And how long would she last with no money and no one to help them? Besides, she didn't want to run from the law; she never had.

She simply wanted her son.

Ethan's thick exhalation echoed beyond the fabric barrier forming the back of the display. "No, I understand. I was just caught off guard." A pregnant pause caused Lindy's palms to sweat while she wondered what Candace said on the other end. She brushed her hands against the soft fabric of her skirt and took a deep, calming breath.

Don't panic. Surely they haven't matched

Lindy Burnett to Melinda Sue Flinn. She closed her eyes. *Not yet. Please, God, not yet.*

"Why do you think this won't affect the adoption?" His voice, a bit softer now, seemed farther away.

Lindy glanced down at her soft watercolor skirt, the blues and mints and pinks that had caught her eye when they were displayed in the window of Consigning Women making her nauseous now. And she saw that she'd bunched the pretty fabric within her palms and formed a few noticeable wrinkles. But she didn't care— her focus was on Ethan's conversation that could very well change her life.

The boiled egg and buttered toast she'd eaten for breakfast threatened to make a hasty exit as he expressed her deepest fears.

"So you're certain that no judge would give her rights back?"

She emitted a barely audible gasp, though she wanted to scream. She *did* deserve her rights back. She'd done everything she could to protect Jerry, had continually put herself between her husband and her child to contain Gil's rage.

The memory of her baby's screams—and that sickening moment of silence—pierced her heart like a jagged knife. That one time, on the night Gil died, she hadn't been able to protect her son.

But she'd tried. She'd truly tried.

"Okay." Ethan's voice seemed calm again, assured that everything would be all right. "Yeah, I understand. But I want you to talk to the folks who decided I had to wait until the end of the summer to adopt Jerry and see if that can be altered now. The quicker I can adopt him, the sooner we can make sure he isn't given back to her. She didn't protect him then. Why would any court believe she'd behave differently now?"

Because I did the best I could then. And I would protect him now. I would die for him.

"No, I don't want to stop pursuing the adoption. Jerry needs my protection more than ever now."

His protection?

Ethan disconnected, and Lindy waited for him to return to the display area. She couldn't help herself. As soon as he pushed the curtain aside and stepped in, she asked, "Why would Jerry need your protection?"

He slid his cell into his jeans pocket. "I'm sorry you had to overhear that. He's fine, or he will be, as soon as I adopt him. But he has an extremely painful past, and unfortunately..." He paused while Lindy held her breath, waiting to see what he'd say about her.

Ethan's gaze shifted to the window. "Look, they're coming."

She twisted around to see the Willow's Haven group crossing the square in a direct path for the store. Kids of all ages were laughing and chatting, shoving at each other the way kids do when they're excited and happy. Another group of adults had gathered a short distance away from the store's entrance, probably the mentors waiting for the children they would be paired with for the Fishers of Men program.

Lindy scanned the crowd of kids until she spotted the preschoolers with Savvy, smiling and waving her hands as she talked animatedly to the smallest children. Most of the little ones nodded, clapped, grinned or laughed as they made their way toward the store. Jerry, however, walked somberly, keeping away from the cluster and on the opposite side of Savvy.

Did he fear all adults?

"There he is." Ethan pushed the fabric aside and extended a hand toward Lindy. "I don't want to talk about that phone conversation now. I'll tell you about it later. Right now I want to spend time with Jerry and remind him of how life will be when that adoption goes through. I can't believe how much I missed him after just meeting him once. I guess it's because I've been praying for him for so long."

"You've been praying for him?" she asked, baffled.

"Every day for three years." His hand remained outstretched, and she couldn't find a reason not to accept it.

She wanted to tell him how very much *she'd* missed Jerry, and how *she'd* prayed for him each and every day since the moment she learned she was pregnant, but she swallowed past the urge, placed her hand in his and allowed him to help her exit the display area. "Thank you."

"Of course." His smile inched up and he squeezed her hand, only slightly, but still...

Lindy did her best to ignore the comfort his warm palm provided and the reminder of the way people typically touched throughout a normal day. For the past three years, she'd done her best to keep from accidentally brushing against a fellow inmate. You never knew when someone might see any physical contact as aggressive and respond in kind, with a punch to the jaw, elbow to the side or worse.

She flinched, suddenly flooded with memories of saying or doing the wrong thing those first few weeks...and ending up in the infirmary. It didn't take her long to learn survival skills for the prison yard.

He held her hand a moment longer than she'd have liked, but she controlled the urge to release it. A normal person wouldn't have a problem with this, and she wanted—needed—to be normal again.

"Lindy, *are* you okay?" he asked, and he sounded like he truly cared.

The answer was simple. No, she wasn't, and she wouldn't be until Jerry was in her life again, for good. She swallowed. "I'm okay."

He nodded, accepting the lie as truth, or deciding to leave it be. Lindy didn't know which, but she was glad that he left it alone and changed the subject.

"Hey, it'll only grow with time, right? That feeling I have toward my son?" He waited a beat for her response, but Lindy couldn't make herself encourage his desire to adopt her boy. Thankfully, the kids and adult mentors neared the door, and she left the question unanswered.

"Come on." He tugged her palm and stepped toward the entrance. "The window looks great, and I know you're probably as anxious to spend time with these kids as I am."

She was anxious to spend time with one child, the same one as Ethan. But there were twenty-four children and an equal number of mentors who needed her help to rent or purchase supplies for the summer fishing program, and she'd meant what she said when she told Mrs. Bowers that they could count on her to do a good job.

"I am anxious." Lindy finally slid her hand from his. As much as she hated to admit it, in order to spend more time with Jerry, she had to spend some with Ethan, too. But she'd keep the physical contact to the bare minimum. Something about him rattled her senses, in the same way Gil had thrown her world off balance when they'd first met so long ago. An extremely intense, but extremely unwanted, attraction.

Ethan was equally charming and equally handsome, if not more, than her husband had been. And he, like Gil, seemed nice, sincere. Honest. But Lindy had become an expert in misguided trust during her marriage, and even more of an authority after the murder that ended it. She'd trusted Marsha as a confidant, the only person who knew how terribly Gil had treated her…and the only one she'd called that night when she'd left her husband sleeping and went searching for the women's shelter.

While Paul had murdered Gil.

"This is going to be a day to remember," Ethan said, his eyes lighting up with excitement at the group of children dashing toward the door. "And I'm not letting anything steal my joy at spending time with Jerry."

"A day to remember," she said at the exact moment Jolaine Bowers reached the front of the store.

"I got a text from Savvy saying they're almost here." She peered through the window. "Look, there they are! Here, Lindy—" she hurriedly handed her a stack of papers "—we can give each mentor a supply list to get them started. I can't wait to see if they like all the new things we got in for this. I'm so excited about the Fishers of Men program. Such a wonderful way to show these kids how much the community cares, don't you think?"

"Definitely," Lindy and Ethan said in unison. He smiled at the moment. So did Mrs. Bowers. Lindy, however, clutched the stack of papers to her chest, stepped toward the door—away from the man unnerving her—and welcomed the crowd.

God, let my little boy see how much I care.

Ethan watched as one by one, a child was paired with an adult to begin the shopping adventure. As much as he hadn't looked forward to the actual fishing, he'd been waiting for *this* moment all weekend: spending time with Jerry as they selected items for Fishers of Men.

Truthfully, he'd also looked forward to seeing Lindy Burnett again. In spite of being burned so badly in the past, he'd found himself thinking about the captivating woman the whole time he'd been away from Claremont. She was so quiet, so reserved, and undeniably troubled by whatever had happened in her past that led her to Claremont with no family, no friends and no job.

She disappeared within the flood of adults and kids grabbing the supply lists, but as one very tall gentleman moved out of the way, Ethan saw her, looking a little rattled but politely answering their questions. She pushed a long strawberry curl away from her face and scanned the crowd as though looking for someone. Ethan suddenly wondered whether that long spiral was as soft as it looked and recalled how badly he'd wanted to push those locks away and see her face a few moments ago.

Then their eyes connected, and he gave her a thumbs-up.

He expected a smile, an acknowledgment that she'd been searching for him, but her eyebrows dipped, her confusion at the friendly gesture evident, and then she continued handing out sheets and answering questions.

What had happened to her in the past? And

why couldn't he stop the desire to right not only Jerry's world, but also hers?

"There's Mr. Ethan." Savvy's words took his attention off the puzzling, riveting female on the other side of the store and onto the freckle-faced boy who had consumed his thoughts and prayers for three years. Oh, how he wanted to adopt Jerry Flinn.

Jerry *Green*. Ethan couldn't wait until this guy shared his name.

He crouched to eye level with his future son. "Hey there, buddy. Remember me?"

Jerry chewed his lower lip and nodded. "Yes, sir. You gave me bread for the birds and said we'd go fishing."

"That's right," Ethan said, delighted to have already gotten more communication today than the entire time they'd spent together on Friday. But still, Jerry's words were spoken hesitantly, as if more out of fear of not answering than in a desire to interact.

No problem. As the social worker had reminded him, it would take time to overshadow the damage that'd been done by Gil Flinn, and potentially some of the placements that had occurred in the foster system over the past three years. But Ethan had time, and he would convince this little guy that he was safe with him. He had to.

"Well, I sure remember you, and I'm excited about us fishing together." He *was* excited about fishing with Jerry, even if he had doubts about fishing in general.

"You're excited, too, aren't you, Jerry?" Savvy prompted. "Last night, at our devotional by the fire pit, Jerry said he wanted to learn to fish."

"Really?" Ethan asked, still crouched so that he saw clearly the play of emotions across the little boy's face. Jerry didn't necessarily want to communicate, but he also didn't want to be rude. Or maybe, as Ethan had suspected before, he'd been taught detrimental consequences if he didn't answer adults. "Well, I'm glad you want to fish." Hoping to keep the conversation going, he asked, "How was your weekend?"

He blinked his blue eyes, the uncertainty he'd seen in Lindy's eyes a few moments ago mirrored in the child's. "It was okay."

Ethan wasn't ready to give up. "Did you make any new friends?" he prodded.

"Jerry, tell Mr. Ethan who you sat with at church yesterday, and at the devotion last night." Savvy pressed her palms together at her chest then clasped her fingers as she spoke. "And we went on that hike Saturday. You had some new friends with you for that, too, didn't you?"

He glanced to Savvy and then to Ethan while

his mouth slid to the side. "I don't remember." Worried eyes looked to Ethan and then at the floor.

The blatant fear in the child punched Ethan in the gut. Had he looked that fearful when he was young, when he'd been thrown from one bad situation to another? But this wasn't a bad situation for Jerry. In fact, it would be a very good one. He merely had to convince the scared boy in front of him that he had no reason to be afraid. "Hey, I forget names all the time." Ethan dipped his head and then looked up to catch Jerry's gaze. When their eyes met, he smiled. "That's fine. We'll learn their names while we fish with them this summer. Sound good?"

Freckles danced as his cheeks lifted a little, and he nodded. "Yes, sir."

"Did you get a list of supplies yet?" Savvy asked.

"I got one last week, but I forgot to bring it with me this morning." He answered Savvy, but directed the words to Jerry. "Why don't we go get one from Miss Lindy, so we can get started?" He noticed that Mrs. Bowers actually stood closer to them and had a stack, too, but he was curious how Lindy was faring at her new job. And he just liked being around the captivating lady.

Standing, he held out a hand toward Jerry.

His mouth flattened for a second, but then he placed his palm against Ethan's and let him guide him through the store toward the strawberry blonde currently answering all the questions from mentors and children.

"Yes, we have more blue fishing rods in the back. Mr. Bowers is there with the additional supplies if you want to go get one from him." She answered the question, but her eyes had caught Ethan's and then her gaze dropped to Jerry, even though she continued responding to those surrounding her. "I'll refill that bin as soon as I can, sir, but we also have the sponge bait in the front of the store near the display window." She looked as though she would speak to Ethan, but then fielded yet another question. "Yes, the live bait can be purchased at the fishing hole. We'll have minnows and worms."

As Ethan and Jerry wedged their way toward the busy lady, she shifted to face them directly. Then she tuned out the others still firing off questions, gathered the papers against her chest and leaned toward the boy beside him. "Hey, Jerry. Are you excited about fishing?"

"I...think so." He tilted his head and squinted up at her, and Ethan noticed her eyes soften and mouth tremble, as though she knew how much this boy had been hurt before and how important it was to show him that he didn't need to fear all adults.

Why would Jerry need your protection?

Ethan recalled her question and knew that, even though she didn't know Jerry's situation, she'd determined that he'd been through difficult times. He could see it clearly in the way she looked at him and spoke to him now, as though she wanted desperately to help.

"Did you get your list of supplies yet?" she asked, placing a palm against the papers at her chest.

Jerry shook his head, and Ethan answered. "That's what we were coming to see you for."

She looked toward Miss Jolaine, standing only a few feet from where Ethan and Jerry had been, and then back to Ethan, but didn't acknowledge that he'd been caught. "Okay, then." She slipped one of the pages free and handed it to Ethan.

"Thanks," he said, then added, "Maybe you can help us find the items?"

"Miss Lindy, can you help me untangle this?" one of the other kids called, holding up two fishing rods with lures hooked together.

"Sure." She touched Jerry's hand. "I'm glad I got to see you again today, Jerry. And I think you're going to love learning to fish." Then she looked at Ethan. "I need to untangle those, but

I can help you find everything on the list after I'm done."

Ethan knew where every item was located. He'd seen most of them last week and the newer things this morning, when he'd helped her with the display. In other words, he wasn't sure why he'd asked for help. Except that he wanted, for some bizarre reason, to spend more time with the beautiful, troubled lady. Which was exactly why he *shouldn't* spend more time with her. "I'm sure we can find it."

Did she look disappointed, or did he imagine it?

"Okay then," she said softly, touching a finger to Jerry's hair before turning and walking toward the boy with the tangled lures.

Jerry looked at Lindy, who was gently unraveling the fishing line as she kindly explained to the other boy how to hook the lure to the side to keep it from happening again. "She's…nice."

Here he was, determined to teach this little boy that he didn't need to fear all adults, and Lindy, a woman with presumably her own share of trouble in her past, had knocked a tiny chip in his wall. How could he maintain his distance from the lady, when she might prove to be a key to getting his future son past his fear?

"Yes," he conceded, "She is."

Chapter Five

The cottage that composed the on-site store at the fishing hole resembled the gingerbread houses Lindy had decorated with her grandmother each Christmas throughout her youth. Painted a cheery yellow, it had white, scalloped cake-icing trim along the roof's edge and seafoam shutters bordering every window. A bright red door bracketed by sizable clay pots with equally vibrant red geraniums formed the entrance. And wooden rocking chairs, in alternating hues of seafoam and turquoise, surrounded the wraparound porch.

When she'd first heard about the fishing hole, Lindy envisioned a small area, probably along a creek, where people sat beneath spindly trees on flat, uncomfortable rocks as they fished. She certainly hadn't expected anything resembling the postcardworthy perfection greeting her when Mrs. Bowers had first brought her here two days ago.

And yesterday, she'd thanked God repeatedly for providing her with the opportunity to work at a place that so clearly defined His creation, as well as a job that gave her the opportunity to see Jerry. However, since her son was slated for the Monday and Wednesday fishing group, and since today's group of Willow's Haven kids had only purchased supplies on Monday and didn't have their first actual fishing day until today, she hadn't seen him since their shopping trip.

She missed him terribly, even more than she had when she was in prison, because now there actually was a chance that she could have him in her life again, and yet she couldn't tell him, couldn't hold him, couldn't explain why she'd missed his second birthday, or his third, or his fourth.

But life was getting better. Just having the opportunity to view all of this, the huge pond sparkling in the early morning sun, the slick green moss highlighting the water's edge and the cascading willows tossing feathery shadows sporadically along the bank, provided a direct contrast from the dingy gray walls that had surrounded her the past three years.

If she had to sum up this place in a single word, it'd be *breathtaking*. In fact, she'd shown up this morning at six, even though the Willow's Haven group wasn't expected until eight, simply because she wanted a little time to appreciate the scene and pray before her official workday began. She had ample time to finish her duties before the kids arrived, so she got her priorities in order, sat in one of the rockers, closed her eyes and talked to God. She thanked Him for helping her find Jerry and for bringing her here, to Claremont. Then she thanked Him for the phone call she'd received last night from Ted Murrell, who said he'd take her case and honestly believed she had a slim chance to get her son back.

Slim was better than none, and she'd take it.

She visualized the day she'd tell Jerry that she was his mommy, that she loved him dearly and had missed him terribly.

I just met him, and I missed him already. Hard to believe... Ethan's statement from Monday had haunted her ever since, because he sounded like *he'd* truly missed Jerry when they were apart, too. Lindy almost believed him.

Would a court believe him, too?

And the other part of Ethan's proclamation bothered her even more: that he'd been praying for Jerry for three years. *Three years.* The amount of time she'd been incarcerated. But he said he'd just met him last week.

Why had he been praying for her little boy?

She kept her eyes closed and prepared to pray more. But, as was often the case, the memory of her sentencing stabbed her heart, and she had to fight off the impulse to question God, like she had so many times, about why He'd allowed her to go to prison in the first place.

Then, because she knew He could read her heart anyway, she asked.

God, why? Why did I have to go through all of that? Why did I lose those precious years with my son?

And since she was already telling Him her heart, she let the base of the matter come to the surface, too…

And since Marsha, the only friend I'd had since high school and the one person I'd entrusted with the truth of Gil's abuse, helped send me to prison, how am I ever going to trust anyone again?

"This place is amazing, isn't it?"

One hand flew to her chest and the other grabbed the wooden armrest as the incredibly beautiful man who planned to take Jerry away climbed the porch steps.

He wore a pale blue short-sleeved shirt unbuttoned over a white T-shirt and khaki shorts, his wavy dark hair a little more mussed than she'd seen it before, and his smile even brighter than usual. He looked as though he belonged in the center of this picturesque place. The perfect man every girl would dream of, relaxing on a blanket beneath one of those willow trees, sharing a picnic with her. They'd be laughing. Enjoying each other's company.

Disarmingly handsome, Ethan Green appeared as though he was completely unaware of the beauty God had bestowed on him. Moreover, he looked undeniably comfortable in his surroundings and totally content in his life.

Like a man who would make an excellent father.

Lindy's throat pinched tight, and a wave of sudden nausea caused her to tense. Why would any jury think she'd be better for Jerry than him?

"Whoa, now." He held up his palms. "Hey, I'm sorry. Seems like I keep managing to sneak up on you, but I promise, that wasn't my intention." He tilted his head and studied her face, which she assumed had gone pale, her freckles probably standing out even more than usual.

"I'm okay," she managed.

He didn't buy it. "Well, you don't look okay. You look like you're going to get sick. Do you need some water or something? And didn't you hear me drive up?"

She patted her hand against her chest and

forced her heartbeat to decrease. It wasn't as if she could explain that she'd spent the last thirty-six months in a place where being taken by surprise could very well mean you'd end up on a gurney...or in a morgue. "I didn't hear you. I guess I was lost in my thoughts." *Lost in my prayers, and in my fears about you.*

"I can see how that'd be easy to do out here." He inhaled deeply and let it out slowly, which unfortunately brought her attention to the wide planes of his chest pressing against the soft fabric of his T-shirt. Then he scanned his surroundings with obvious appreciation, giving her another smile that sent a wave of something that definitely wasn't nausea through her before sitting in the next rocker. Way too close for comfort. "This place is incredible," he said.

"Yes, it is." Lindy couldn't fathom why he'd shown up this early and suddenly regretted taking a moment to relax on the porch. It'd be easier to stay away from him if she were working on the start-up list that Mrs. Bowers had provided. She'd seen his name slated for the first group this morning and had been eager to start her workday spending time with Jerry, but the Willow's Haven bus wouldn't arrive at the fishing hole until eight. She checked the time on her watch. "It's just past seven. The kids won't be here for another hour."

"I know, but I've been up since five." He settled into the rocker, extended a long leg to the porch rail then pushed back to gently rock, as though he planned to sit here beside her, truly closer than she'd like, for a while. "I'm staying at the Claremont Bed and Breakfast, and the couple who runs the place start cooking before dawn. When those scents—bacon, eggs, sausage gravy, biscuits—hit my room each morning... Let me tell you, for a single guy, it's like waking up and thinking you might be in heaven." He grinned. "I didn't want to insult them or anything, so I got up and ate."

"That was mighty polite of you." She wished his smile didn't affect her the way it did, making her stomach flutter and her skin warm and tempting her to smile in return, but she held the instinct in check. She'd mastered hiding her emotions over the past three years, and she wasn't about to lose control of that ability now, especially not with Ethan Green. She didn't need to encourage this man. Or any man, for that matter.

He gave her a one-shoulder shrug and a wink. "What can I say? I do what I can."

Lindy couldn't deny he was charming, but Gil had been charming, too, for a while. "That still doesn't explain why you came out here so early." She'd planned on slowly working through the small list of daily tasks that Jolaine had given her, but now that Ethan sat nearby, she decided to do her best to stay busy for the remainder of their time alone.

Alone. With Ethan Green. Again. The guy who, in spite of the fact that he could take her son away, still reminded her of how it felt to be around a man and notice all of those masculine traits that rattled her senses. Strong jaw. Broad shoulders. Muscled biceps and forearms sprinkled with hair, slightly tanned, probably from working outside around his house. Then there were the masculine hands that currently relaxed against his rocker's armrests, but that looked capable of pretty much anything. Legs that stretched all the way out to the porch rail, much farther than she'd reach.

Her eyes were suddenly drawn to his extended knee, and an angry, spiderlike scar that wrapped its way completely around it. What had happened? A car wreck? Or some other kind of accident?

Apparently her face showed her surprise because she realized she'd been caught staring at it.

He dropped the leg from the porch rail, sat a little straighter in the rocker and said, "I came early because I'm excited about seeing Jerry, and I was anxious to get out here to see the place."

Okay. So asking about the scar was off-limits. And she shouldn't ask anyway. She didn't want to have *that* kind of relationship with the man, didn't want to act overly interested. Because she wasn't. Really. The only reason she'd even interact with him was because of his mentorship of her son. She swallowed, pushed the question about the scar out of her mind and instead focused on casual conversation. "Yes, it's beautiful here. And the weather is very comfortable, especially with that breeze." She nodded toward the willows swaying in the distance.

He started rocking again, taking another long, appreciative gaze of the impressive view. "The Tingles, the couple who own the B and B, said this place was nice, but this goes way beyond nice. And I have to admit, if I'd known a fishing hole could look like this, I'd have taken up the sport years ago."

"I'm pretty sure they don't all look like this." Suddenly needing to end this one-on-one time with the man who intended to take her son, Lindy pushed up from the rocker. "I've got a few things to get done before the bus arrives." She started toward the pebbled parking area and noticed a shiny navy SUV parked next to her small, dented car. Even their vehicles showed which one of them had more to offer a child.

"I'll help you." And then, before she had a chance to protest, those long legs carried him right beside her, eluding her attempt to get as far away from him as possible.

"I can handle it." The words came out in a rush due to the nerves he rattled, and she refused to look at him or encourage him in any way. Instead, she hoped he would pivot toward the cottage and return to his rocker until the kids arrived.

He didn't even pause, but continued walking beside her. Then, when she reached for the back door handle, he stopped her, his warm palm and long fingers touching her forearm and gently turning her so that she had no choice but to look into those intoxicating chocolate eyes.

Lindy was rocked to her core by the truth. This man not only had the power to take her son, but he also had the power to crush her heart in the process.

God, please help me control this bizarre feeling. The last thing I need in my life is another man letting me down. Especially the one trying to take Jerry.

She opened her mouth to tell him again that she didn't need his help, but she didn't get the chance.

"Lindy, don't. Don't keep trying to do everything on your own." He shook his head subtly as his eyes connected with hers. "I don't know what's happened in your past, who made you so fearful of people who want to help, but I promise you, that's what I'm trying to do—help. Let me do that, okay? We're going to be seeing each other fairly regularly with this whole fishing gig, and I've noticed— The thing is, it seems like Jerry comes out of his shell around you."

Her knees were a little wobbly, either from his proximity, the way his hand still rested on her forearm or his words about her son. She'd thought she wanted to get some distance from him, but hope ebbed through to her very soul at his observation, and she found herself asking, "You noticed he comes out of his shell around me?"

Did she and Jerry still have a semblance of that bond they'd made way back when?

And what would Ethan do if he ever figured out why?

"I did. Jerry is comfortable around you, and I want him to be that comfortable around me, too. I mean, he's going to be the biggest part of my life really soon."

She didn't like the sound of that at all. She slid her arm away from his, then turned to begin gathering the quilts from her backseat.

"What does that have to do with letting you help me out?"

Mrs. Bowers had laundered all of the patchwork quilts that they provided for folks fishing at the pond, and three stacks of them filled her backseat. It was way more than she could carry in a single trip. And he noticed, sliding beside her to grab the second batch before she had a chance to close the car door with her hip. Which made her notice the crisp scent of his aftershave, even more intoxicating than the floral scent of fabric softener wafting from the quilts.

Truly, the fabric softener wasn't even a close second to the scent of Ethan Green.

"Just see it as my way of thanking you," he said, and she pressed her face closer to the quilts to take in more of the fabric softener smell…and less of the man tempting her senses.

She walked swiftly toward the large cedar chests on the front porch where the quilts were stored. "Thanking me for what?" He got to the chests first and lifted the lid on one.

She was grateful for the sweet scent of cedar spilling from the chest, and the fact that it overpowered every other smell around.

Lindy suddenly recalled the hope chest her grandmother had given her when she turned thirteen. The one she'd filled with all the typical things a teenager thinks she might need when she gets married. Gil hadn't liked the cedar scent of the items that she'd stored inside so, wanting to make him happy, she'd ended up selling all the sentimental contents at their first yard sale.

She'd cried all night after.

"Lindy, are you okay?"

Why did he keep asking her that? "I'm fine."

And why did she keep answering with a lie?

Because she knew the truth. The pain of her past, not only the prison time but also the time she'd spent with a man who had no qualms about hitting her when she didn't behave the way he wanted, had made her far from "fine."

He gave her the look she'd seen from him before, the one that said he knew she wasn't being completely forthright, but he wouldn't press the issue. She thanked God for that small favor. And *that* reminded her that Ethan had never answered her question. "You said you were helping me as a thank you. Thanking me for what?"

"For helping my little man open up." He closed the lid on the chest. "Because by helping him, you're helping me."

"How's that?" she asked as they made their way back to the car.

"You'll help me get closer to my son, and I'll be able to adopt him before…"

She stopped walking just shy of the car door, turned and asked, "Before what?"

"Before something happens that would cause him to be hurt again." He moved past her, leaned into the car to retrieve the quilts that were farther away and bring them out on his own. Meanwhile Lindy tried to formulate the words to ask what he was talking about, preferably without giving away too much.

Before she could say a thing, he asked, "Did you need anything else from the car?"

She shook her head and decided to see just how much he knew about her son's past. And hers. "Jerry's been hurt?" Then she held her breath and waited to see how he'd answer.

He nudged the door shut. "He has, but I'm going to do my best to prove to him that he can trust again and show him what a parent *should* be."

Lindy walked alongside him toward the cottage, while trying to figure out how she'd ever compete with this seemingly perfect man in court. She knew how a parent should be, and that was the kind of parent she'd always wanted to be to her son. The kind of parent she would be if given another chance.

Would a court believe her?

Since his arms were filled with the quilts, she moved ahead of him and opened the next cedar chest for him to place them inside. "Thanks," he said, and again threw her off balance just by standing so near and appearing so nice.

Lindy still needed to get the rental equipment ready inside the store, but they had a little more time, and she wanted to know...

"The other day you said Jerry needed protection. And today you said he'd been hurt." She moved toward the red door, just in case his words caused an emotion she didn't want him to see, and attempted to ask another question without letting on how very much she wanted to know what Ethan would say. "Who does he need protection from?"

"His mother." The answer was delivered matter-of-factly, as if there were no doubt in his mind. He might as well have punched her in the stomach like one of those women in prison had.

Her hand tightened on the doorknob. What *had* he been told? And what did he believe? What would a judge and jury believe? "His mother hurt him?"

"Yes," he said. "Not personally, or at least not from what the courts could tell, but she didn't stop him from being hurt, either. And I'm going to do my best to keep him from being hurt again."

A low rumble in the distance caused both of them to turn and see the noisy school bus slowly creeping along the gravel drive with several pickup trucks and cars following.

"That's them. I'm going to get my gear." He left the porch and headed toward his SUV.

Lindy didn't respond, but kept her eyes peeled on that approaching bus, the one that held her son. Ethan said he planned to do his best to keep him from being hurt again.

She believed him.

A court probably would, too.

But somehow, she—and her new attorney—had to convince them all that *she* wanted to keep him from being hurt again, too.

Ethan and Jerry were scheduled for two hours of fishing this morning, and an hour and a half in, they still hadn't gotten a single nibble. Or at least one that counted. Their bait had been swiped a few times, but with no fish to show for the effort. And Ethan was clueless about how to fix the problem.

A cheer from a short distance away caused him—and his little man—to turn and watch, again, as more of their peers found success in the pond.

"They got one," Jerry said glumly. But still, he was sitting by Ethan, communicating with him and sharing a father-son activity with him.

So Ethan couldn't be that disappointed that they hadn't yet mastered this whole fishing thing.

"Yeah, they got one." He turned to look at the little boy beside him instead of their red-and-white bobbers floating on the water. "Pretty cool, huh? Hey, maybe we'll get one soon, too."

Jerry sat beside him on one of the patchwork quilts Ethan had helped Lindy with earlier and squinted up at him. "We haven't got one yet." It wasn't the first time he'd said this.

"That's true." Ethan looked back to the bobbers just in time to see Jerry's jiggle, making tiny waves in the surface. "But hey, we may have one now. Look!"

Jerry turned as the floating sphere disappeared into the water. "I got one!"

"Pull it up and see," Ethan encouraged him, hoping it would be one of those small speckled fish that everyone else seemed to be catching.

Jerry jerked the red fishing rod, yanking the line out of the water and the empty shiny gold hook at the end mocked them. "Aw," he sighed, his tiny shoulders lifting and dropping. "We got nothing. Again."

If this was an ordinary occurrence, the two of them spending a morning together trying to catch a fish, their lack of success might have been funny, something they would tease each other about and laugh at, but this wasn't an ordinary occurrence, at least not yet. Ethan had really hoped they would find themselves cheering, too, like the woman and little girl on the opposite side of the pond who had apparently caught *another* fish and were now doing a celebratory dance.

Jerry blew out another breath of disappointment.

Okay. So Ethan hadn't thought he knew anything about fishing, and clearly, he'd been right. But he didn't want this first attempt of a happy memory with his future son to go down as a total failure. And it hadn't been a complete loss, since Jerry had seemed to enjoy their time tossing the practice sponge bait into the water and reeling it in. However, if Ethan had known that would be the best part of the experience, he would have extended their practice time to an hour, instead of merely the first ten minutes.

"You know—" he glanced at his watch and saw they had fifteen minutes until the kids would head back to Willow's Haven on the bus "—I think we've given it a good effort today, and I'm pretty sure I saw some fruit Popsicles in the freezer at the store up there. Wanna go get one?"

Jerry glanced toward yet another pair clapping in the distance, then at the water in front of them, and then back at Ethan. "Sure."

Ethan had thought the Popsicle offer would take his mind off the finicky fish, but he could tell that the little boy had really wanted to experience the same excitement his friends had this morning. "We'll get a fish next time." He sure hoped he wasn't lying.

"Okay," Jerry said, visibly unconvinced, which made Ethan regret the statement. How many adults had promised the boy something and then fallen short of delivering?

God, I know nothing is too small for You. So when we come back on Monday, can You help us catch a fish? Help me figure out what I'm doing wrong here.

Jerry placed his rod beside his tiny tackle box, which held nothing more than bobbers and sponge bait, since they were using minnows Ethan had purchased from Lindy at the store. Then he opened the lid of their small minnow bucket and watched the tiny bait fish swimming madly around the water.

Ethan peeked in, too. "They didn't do their job today catching fish for us, did they?"

Jerry shook his head and dropped the Styrofoam lid back in place. "No, sir. They sure didn't."

"We'll get some next time," he assured Jerry again—and then said another quick prayer that he was telling the truth. "Come on, let's go see what flavors of Popsicles they have." He tousled Jerry's hair, gave him a smile and was rewarded when the right corner of the little boy's mouth lifted, sending a sprinkle of freckles dancing on his cheek.

They passed several pairs of adults and children fishing on their way to the store. Ethan had already gotten to know a few of the mentors, and he took the chance now to say hello and ask how they were faring with their attempts at catching anything. Most had caught plenty, except for one pair who had only caught one bream, which Ethan now recognized as the name of the small speckled fish the group was searching for.

He waited for Jerry to speak to any of the other kids they met along the way, but he didn't say a word. Then again, neither did most of the other kids. Maybe they had all arrived at Willow's Haven after sad situations and were having as difficult of a time interacting with others as Jerry. Or maybe they were merely concentrating on the task at hand, more concerned with catching fish before their time was up than communicating.

But as Ethan and Jerry passed the last fishing pair before reaching the store, Ethan noticed that the mentor wasn't quite an adult yet. It was Brodie and Savvy Evans's teenage son,

Dylan, whom Ethan had met when the group shopped for gear on Monday. Dylan, an outgoing kid with an obvious appreciation for life in general, leaned back on his quilt and gave Jerry a playful grin. "Hey there, Jerr-Bear, how's it going?"

Jerry stopped walking, flipped his small hands upside down to display empty palms, and explained, "We didn't catch nothing."

Dylan laughed. "Hey, that happens to me sometimes. Actually, it happened to me the last time I was here." He leaned a little closer to Jerry. "You know what my dad used to tell me about those days when you don't catch anything?"

Jerry shook his head, then he raised his eyebrows and opened his eyes wider to hear what the older, wiser kid had to say.

"He said that sometimes those fish pick who they want to play hide-and-seek with, and today they must have picked you." Dylan playfully pointed a finger toward Jerry.

Jerry's lip quirked to the side, his eyes squinting a little as he processed this. Then he looked up at Ethan and asked, "Will they play hide-and-seek again next time?"

Dylan laughed, and Ethan answered, "I sure hope not."

"Me, too," Jerry said. He didn't look quite

as disappointed as before, though. Ethan would need to learn ways to help his little boy cope with the disappointments in life. He supposed that was all part of parenting, and he'd wade through those challenges as they came. But for now he was thankful that Dylan had found a way to lift Jerry's spirits.

Then again, Ethan had thought of the Popsicles. He looked toward the store and saw Lindy, standing on the porch watching them, her hand resting against her chest the way he'd noticed her do a few times before, as though she were moved by whatever held her attention.

And at this moment, that seemed to be Ethan and his little man.

Lindy. Something else positive in their day. She seemed so mesmerized with ordinary life, which again caused Ethan to wonder exactly what hers had been like before he met the beautiful lady that first day in the Claremont square. And before he'd found himself thinking about her on a regular basis ever since.

"There's Miss Lindy," Jerry said, the hint of enthusiasm in his voice matching what Ethan found himself feeling every time he saw her.

"Yep, there she is," he agreed, noticing the way the sun highlighted the red-blond waves that tumbled past her shoulders. Today she wore a creamy yellow sleeveless top paired with a multicolored floral skirt and sandals. Most of the women he'd seen today at the fishing hole had on shorts, or capris, or cutoff jeans. But Lindy stood out from all of them in the beautiful, feminine clothes.

Then again, she stood out from all of them anyway. She was so incredibly stunning, as though she were painted into this picturesque scene instead of actually a part of it. There was just something about her that held his interest and made him never want to look away.

Ethan watched her attention land on the little guy beside him, the smile that mesmerized him obviously meant for Jerry rather than him.

Ethan shook away the odd pang of disappointment that she didn't seem to have a smile for him. He wasn't looking for any kind of relationship again, not after what happened with Jenny, but he couldn't deny that he'd visualized Lindy Burnett smiling at him that way too.

"So, did y'all catch anything, Jerry?" she asked. Yup, her focus was definitely on the child, not the man.

"No, ma'am," he said, "but Mr. Ethan said we're going to get some Popsicles anyway."

And with that, her gaze moved from Jerry to Ethan, and he saw a hint of appreciation in her eyes that went straight to his heart.

Amazing what a little appreciation from a gorgeous woman did for a guy's ego.

"Good idea," she said. "The Popsicles are in that freezer inside. What flavor do you want, Jerry? We have strawberry, grape, peach and pineapple. But you'll want to make sure you wash your hands first. You've been touching those minnows, right?"

Jerry gave her a lopsided grin. "They're slippery."

She laughed, a soft, lilting sound that also teased Ethan's heart. "Yes, they are. And that means you definitely want to wash those hands. The sink is at the back of the store. There's one just for kids. And there's some of that foaming soap beside it. You'll want to use plenty of that."

"Yes, ma'am," he answered, then went inside, while Ethan stood, once again taken aback by the natural beauty and undeniable intrigue of the woman on the porch.

"No fish?" she asked softly.

"Not today," he answered, glad for another opportunity to communicate with her. "And I'll be honest, I have no idea what we're doing wrong. We have the same bait as everyone else, and we're all fishing at the same pond. I can't understand why they seem to be hitting everyone else's lines instead of ours." He glanced toward the lake, where he saw one little fisherman holding up a bream and grinning toward his mentor. Ethan had so hoped to have that moment with Jerry today.

Her teeth ran over her lower lip, as though she debated what she wanted to say.

"What is it?" he asked. "If you know of something I'm doing wrong, I'd sure love to figure it out. I want this experience to be great for my little guy. Gotta tell you, I hated hearing all of his disappointed sighs every time we saw someone else with a bream on the line."

"Bless his heart," she whispered, peeking through the store window to see Jerry, moving from the sink to the freezer. "Maybe you should try fishing in one of the shady spots next time."

"A shady one?" He looked toward the pond and saw their blanket and equipment still in their spot, near the center of the right side of the pond. Away from any of the cascading willows. There had been an early rain this morning that put a cool breeze in the air, and Ethan had picked the place because it hadn't been overly hot, and he thought Jerry would enjoy sitting in the morning sun. But now he saw that the majority of mentors had selected spots near or under the trees. In fact, the only other pair that were completely in the sun were the ones who had only caught one bream. "Why are they all in the shady spots?"

She placed a crooked finger over her mouth to attempt to hide a grin, then slid her hand away. "Maybe because that's where the fish are?"

"Seriously?" he asked.

Her mouth still fought an impulse to grin, and it made her even more appealing. And made him focus on that heart-shaped mouth. *What would it be like to...*

"Typically, the fish gravitate toward the shade, or logs, or submerged trees. Things like that," she said, and Ethan pushed the unwanted thought away. Then she tilted her head and asked, "You really haven't been fishing before?"

"Never had anyone to take me," he said, before realizing just how much that gave away about his past. He wasn't thinking straight, probably because he couldn't get his mind off what it'd be like to kiss Lindy Burnett.

Her eyebrows dipped, that pretty mouth drew downward and Ethan sensed that she might be feeling pity toward him. It was not what he wanted. At all.

"Not that I ever had any inclination for fishing," he clarified. "I probably wouldn't have liked it that much anyway." He forced a grin, but her questioning gaze told him she wasn't buying it.

"My grandmother taught me," she said.

"Your grandmother? Taught you to fish?" He'd have thought her father, or maybe her mother, but not her grandma. Everything about this lady was unique.

"My grandmother raised me," she said, and then added, "My mother had me when she was very young and didn't want to raise a baby as a teen. She left right after I was born."

"You don't see her?"

"Never have," she said, as though it were no big deal. "But she did what was best for me. My grandmother was terrific, and I don't have any complaints about how I grew up."

Which extinguished his guess that her mother was the part of her troubled past that still hurt so deeply now. She didn't seem as though she harbored any bitterness toward her.

So what *had* happened?

Jerry stuck his head out and announced, "I got a strawberry one." He held up the paper-wrapped treat. "Can I eat it now?"

"Sure," Ethan said.

He exited the store and moved toward one of the rockers. "Can I eat it here?"

This time, Lindy answered. "Of course."

"I'll need to pay for that," Ethan said, "and I

think I'll get me one, too." He looked to Lindy. "Which flavor is your favorite?"

"To be honest, I haven't tried one yet." Then, watching Jerry peel the paper away and take a lick, she added, "Actually, it's been a long time since I've had a Popsicle."

"Then I'd say you're due. Which kind do you want? My treat." He grinned. "How much are they, by the way?"

"Just a quarter, but you don't need to get me one. I'll have one later." She moved toward Jerry and sat in the rocker beside him. "You like that, huh?"

Jerry smiled and nodded as he continued eating. "Yes, ma'am."

Ethan went inside, washed his hands and grabbed two Popsicles from the freezer. Then he placed three quarters on the counter and went outside to find her still chatting with Jerry.

"Yeah, sometimes those fish do play hide-and-seek," she said, "but I'm hoping they won't play so well the next time."

"Me, too," he said, nibbling the end of his Popsicle while peering at the alluring lady.

"I got you a peach one," Ethan said, "and put my money on the counter." He extended the Popsicle.

"You didn't have to do that," she said, but she

accepted it and then looked up at him, bright blue eyes glistening. "But thank you."

"It's really good," Jerry said, while Ethan and Lindy peeled their papers away and tasted the cool treats.

Jerry glanced at Ethan, and then watched Lindy as she tried hers. "Do you like it, Miss Lindy?"

She swallowed, then nodded. "I like this," she said, giving him a tender smile. "I like this very much."

Ethan watched her, eating his Popsicle and sitting beside his future son, and he knew she wasn't just talking about the popsicle. She, like Ethan, enjoyed the feeling of sitting on the porch with a little boy, spending time together on a beautiful early summer day.

And he found himself suddenly wondering if what she liked so much about this moment included him.

Chapter Six

Lindy reflected on the sermon she'd heard at church Wednesday night as she filled the green watering can at the fishing hole's cottage on Friday afternoon. The preacher at the Claremont Community Church, Brother Henry, had spoken about new beginnings and second chances, citing the stories of David, Paul, Peter and the Samaritan woman. So many people in the Bible had been given a second chance. It gave Lindy hope.

She felt certain God meant for her to hear that particular sermon, because she truly needed the reminder that He was a God of second chances, and that she might actually get a second chance to have her son in her life.

"Please, Lord, let that happen," she whispered, pouring half of the water over the first pot of geraniums and then emptying the remainder around the stunning red clusters in the second pot.

She'd been a little disappointed when she'd first arrived at the church Wednesday night, because she'd looked forward to seeing the Willow's Haven children filling their respective pews. But she'd learned that the group often held their midweek devotions at the children's home, particularly on pretty nights when the weather permitted them to gather outside.

She'd also learned that the children had an afternoon devotion each day at the home, and had been very grateful that Jerry already had the presence of God in his world. Lindy had grown up going to church and talking freely about God with her grandmother, but Gil hadn't been a believer. She'd married him thinking he would come around in his spirituality, but they'd never stepped foot in a church after their wedding day.

Lindy refilled the watering can and headed to the store's back entrance, where long, slender planters lined the deck. Here, Mrs. Bowers had chosen cascading petunias in deep purple, red and white to provide an intense splash of color.

She refilled the can twice and had only made it halfway down the porch, but she didn't mind. Out here, with the beauty of these flowers, as well as the sparkling pond, feathery willows and brilliant green moss-covered bank, she felt a peace she hadn't experienced in three years.

A child's laughter drifted across the air, and she paused to view the only current guests, a father and son, at the opposite side of the pond. The little boy held up a fish so small that Lindy could barely see it, while the man took a photo with his phone.

Sadness swiftly replaced the peace she'd felt merely seconds ago. She'd so wanted Jerry to have a father like that, but Gil had been a far cry from the type of dad she'd dreamed about for her son. She'd wanted a man who would want to spend time with Jerry, who truly enjoyed being a father and all of the wonderful responsibilities that went along with the role.

Gil had thought of their baby as more of a burden than a blessing.

"Hello? Anybody here?" The deep voice grew louder as a man walked around the store to the back deck. And even though Lindy couldn't see him yet, she recognized Ethan's voice easily. Suddenly finding her palms sweaty, she brushed her free hand against the gauzy fabric of her sundress.

"There you are." He wore a slate blue T-shirt and khaki shorts. As he climbed the stairs of the deck, she realized that he didn't look like any schoolteacher she'd ever known, and Lindy suspected every eighth-grade girl in his class had a crush on their teacher.

"You have a customer," he said, slowly walking toward her on the deck.

"I do? I didn't hear anyone, and I've only been out here a few minutes. I'll go see what they need. I wonder why they didn't ring the bell." She placed the watering can on a nearby table and hurried toward the door, not only wanting to help her customer but also to put a little space between her and the handsome man she'd actually dreamed about last night and who—she had to keep reminding herself—wanted her son.

His laughter halted her progress as she reached for the knob. "What is it?" she asked.

"Your customer," he said, pointing his thumb at himself. "You're looking at him."

"Oh," she said on a sigh. She'd hoped to escape yet another situation where she'd be alone with the guy who could ruin her life. And who, in spite of that blatant fact, still made her wonder what it'd be like to be in his arms.

"Well, you don't sound very excited about it," he said, still grinning. It was a beautiful grin that came naturally, making him appear honest and approachable. Trustworthy. In fact, Lindy's resistance to trust slipped a little whenever he was around.

A judge would fall in love with him as the ideal parent. A woman who didn't protect her heart could fall in love with him, too.

Lindy had to protect her heart.

"No, it's not that," she lied. Again. And mentally noted that the majority of her conversations with this guy ended up with at least one prevarication on her part. And with her asking God for forgiveness. Which she did now. Again.

But she didn't need to justify her odd reaction. Instead, she asked, "Did you ring the bell?"

"No, I figured you were nearby and decided to find you on my own. But I didn't sneak up on you this time, right? You didn't even jump."

"That's right, you didn't. Thank you for that." He hadn't wanted to startle her. As much as she didn't want to like the things he did, Lindy appreciated the thoughtfulness behind the gesture.

"You're welcome." He moved toward the tiny table and picked up the watering can. "Need some help watering the flowers?"

"No, I can do it." She reached toward the can and, since he held the handle, wrapped her hand around the spout. "Are you going fishing? Did you need to buy some bait or something?" He had said he was a customer, so presumably, he'd meant to make a purchase.

Unless he was here to see her.

Was he here to see her? And how would she feel about that if he was?

Her stomach fluttered, giving her the answer.

He didn't release the can when she put her hand on it, but instead, gently tugged it closer to his chest and grinned. "I wasn't going to point out the obvious, but it looks like you're getting as much water on yourself as the plants."

Lindy glanced down to the gauzy turquoise fabric of the dress she'd fallen in love with at the consignment shop in the square. Apparently, she'd doused herself as she'd been watering the flowers, and she hadn't even noticed. The majority of the fabric from her knees down was soaked. "Oh, my."

"How about I refill the can and finish watering these, and you can fix a minnow bucket for us to use at the pond?"

"For *us* to use?" she asked.

"Us," he said. "Me…and you."

Goose bumps moved up her legs and arms, almost as rapidly as those flutters in her stomach converted to a rapid staccato.

"How does that sound?" he continued, not realizing how very much his statement had pierced her heart. "Us fishing together? I want to get in a little practice before Jerry and I come back on Monday, and you definitely know more about it than I do."

So it wasn't because he wanted to spend time with her necessarily, but because he wanted to practice. Which was good. Really.

Even so, she didn't need to spend any one-on-one time with the guy she couldn't get off her mind. "I'm working." *Keep it short and simple, Lindy. No need to waste words.*

He nodded. "I know, but as far as I can tell, the only other folks fishing seem like they're doing just fine. And we can keep an eye out for any cars that come up." He grinned and added, "Or they can ring the bell. Come on, Lindy," he added softly, temptingly, "spend some time with me."

Exactly what she shouldn't do, and he knew good and well that they wouldn't be able to hear the bell at the pond. "But we wouldn't hear the bell."

"I was joking about that. Don't you think if someone needs you, they'll come find you the way I did? And I'm sure Mr. and Mrs. Bowers expect you to help customers out when they're having a difficult time catching anything."

He was good, she'd give him that. So charismatic that she was having a difficult time remembering why she should say no.

"They'd want you to help me out," he continued.

She pointed out the obvious. "You haven't even tried."

"Sure, I did. For two hours on Wednesday."

He exuded charm without any apparent effort. "You haven't tried *today*."

"No, I haven't, but I don't have a lot of time to sit there and wonder what I'm doing wrong. I told Jerry we'd catch something on Monday, and I've got to make good on that promise. I'm not about to let him down."

Lindy could've been touched by his desire to keep his word, but she was more bothered that he'd *promised* something he wasn't sure he could fulfill. She didn't want Jerry disappointed if Ethan didn't deliver on that promise.

"Wasn't that a bit careless, telling him you would do something when you aren't certain you can?" She couldn't control the accusatory tone; it'd have been just the kind of thing Gil would have done. He was always making promises to Lindy—that things would get better, that he wouldn't hit her again, that he wouldn't hurt her again…

"Yes, it was," Ethan admitted. "And I wish I hadn't said it. But I did."

"You said you were going to do your best to keep him from being hurt again," she reminded him. She'd replayed his statement several times, especially during her talks with her attorney this week, when she'd been reminded how much a judge could be influenced by the possibility of a good father for Jerry.

"I know. I did say that, and I meant it." His tone was resolute.

Lindy had to make him understand. "Promising him something and not following through *would* hurt him." She swallowed hard.

He didn't argue with her, but nodded. "I know that, too. So right now the best thing I can do to keep that from happening is to practice my fishing skills before I bring him here Monday—and pray. I've got the praying part covered, but I figure God wouldn't mind me at least learning more about what I'm doing, too."

She truly wanted to dislike him, but even the way he admitted his mistakes tugged at her heart.

He gently pulled the watering can from her hand. "I saw a water spigot on the side of the house. I'll go fill the can and finish watering the flowers, and you can get a minnow bucket ready for fishing."

"But…" She was sure that Mr. and Mrs. Bowers wouldn't mind her helping a customer fish. In fact, they'd probably encourage it. However, he wasn't any ordinary customer. And she really didn't want to sit on a quilt and fish beside him, spending an afternoon together as if they were a couple instead of two people who were going to find themselves on opposite sides of a courtroom soon.

Even if he didn't know that yet.

"Come on, Lindy," he said, his voice low and intense. "I need your help to keep my promise to him. I honestly don't want to disappoint him in any way, and he wants to catch a fish."

Mr. Murrell's words from their conversation this morning echoed in her thoughts. *The worst thing that could happen is that the judge will find the potential father as undeniably believable. Trustworthy. Someone who would be an exceptional role model for your little boy.*

Ethan Green would be all of those things.

"Come on. It'll be good for you to actually enjoy this place, and there's no denying I need all of the help I can get." When she didn't readily agree, he added, "You could also give me some advice about Jerry."

That got her attention. "Advice about Jerry?"

"You know, a woman's perspective. We've spent the past two mornings together at Willow's Haven, and everything seems to be going fine, but the social worker is coming back next week to check on our interactions and write her report for the court, and I want to make sure she sees how well we're doing."

Jealousy ebbed through her. He'd spent two mornings with her son. They were growing closer. She hadn't spent that much time with Jerry.

But he *did* talk to her on Wednesday. And he'd *smiled*, a few times. In other words, he was doing better already, and undoubtedly Ethan had some part in that. "What kind of advice do you need?" she heard herself ask. "What kind of woman's perspective?"

"Sometimes he shuts down, gets really quiet. Candace, the social worker, said he's always done that. Apparently, he comes out of his shell somewhat, interacts and even seems like everything is going well, but he has moments when they can't figure out what's going on in his mind."

Lindy bit the inside of her lower lip to keep from giving too much away. She hated to think of Jerry so sad. She'd seen him start to come out of his shell on Wednesday, too, had felt very hopeful that he was progressing so quickly, but now she suspected that he'd done that before. And then he'd gotten very sad again.

"And I haven't been able to figure out how to break through that wall when it happens, when he looks so sad and withdrawn," Ethan continued. "Maybe you could help me with that."

"You want me to help you…with Jerry." The thought sounded absurd. Why would she help him get closer to her son? But Ethan had the opportunity to see Jerry more often than she did, and because of that, he also had the opportunity to help Jerry deal with his sadness.

"Don't get me wrong. I can tell he's getting better, talking to me some, which is what Candace said he would do. That's how he normally handles the changes in his life when he gets moved from one place to another. She said he shuts down at first, but then opens up to his new family, and then he has periods of sadness. Those phases are the reason the last family didn't keep him."

Lindy didn't want to think about how many times her little boy had been uprooted, particularly this last time, when a family had said they would give him a forever home…and then changed their mind. He'd had no stability at all. She swallowed, recalling the last moment she'd held him—but an even stronger memory was the moment the officer had pulled her screaming baby from her arms.

"But I want him to trust me, to know I'm

never going to let him down," Ethan said. "So I've got to figure out how to *show* him, because simply telling him isn't going to cut it."

Those chocolate eyes connected with hers, and she could see how sincere he was, how much he already cared about her son. And she suspected Jerry had started caring about him, too, after seeing the two of them interact on Wednesday. So she *had* to help him out. Because she couldn't let her son be disappointed again.

"You're right," she said. "You can't simply tell a little boy something and expect him to believe it at face value. He needs to *see* how much you care."

"I know. So…how do I make that happen?"

She'd made her decision. No way would she let Jerry be hurt again if she could help it, and for now that meant helping Ethan Green grow even closer to her son. "To start with, you don't break any promises. So on Monday, you make certain he catches a fish. Which means today… we practice."

"That's what I was hoping you'd say." His smile lit up his face, and she found herself swaying a little on the way into the cottage. Then mentally slapping herself back to reality once she got inside.

This man might very well take her son away for good.

* * *

Ethan carried the Styrofoam minnow bucket in one hand and their fishing rods in the other as he and Lindy walked toward the pond. He hadn't intended to ask her to help him fish, hadn't intended to spend any more one-on-one time with the attractive lady with the troubled past. In fact, he'd promised himself on the drive over to get the minnows and head to the pond with as little interaction as possible with the woman who caused him to feel the same way he'd felt when he met Jenny.

She'd sat beside him in that very first class on the first day of college. Then they'd laughed when they'd shown up at the next class together...and the next. Their schedules had been identical, as if they'd planned it, and they'd bonded, quickly becoming friends. Then study partners. But they never crossed the boundary into anything more, because the situation had been so perfect. They shared classes, they shared college majors and they were too "alike" to date. But their main difference had been family; she'd had amazing parents, the kind Ethan had only dreamed of. And he'd shared his past with Jenny—how badly the abuse had hurt him, not only physically but emotionally, when he went the remainder of his childhood without experiencing familial love.

Maybe that was why he'd wanted so desperately to comfort her after her parents died suddenly. When she'd heard about the car crash, she'd come to Ethan. And he'd held her when she'd cried. Gotten closer to her as she went through such a difficult time. And over the months that followed, they'd become inseparable.

And they'd fallen in love.

Odd, that a tragedy had brought him closer to anyone than he'd ever been. But it had. And then Jenny had found what she deemed "true love" with Ethan's best friend.

No way could he let himself feel that way again, like he could fall for a woman in a "madly, deeply, forever and ever, till death do us part" way.

It was there, the possibility, hovering in the near distance each time he was around Lindy Burnett. Which was exactly why he'd planned to get the bait and head to the pond.

But then he'd seen her, merely watering flowers on the deck, her long strawberry curls moving in the breeze, her inquisitive face concentrating on him as he neared. Blue eyes squinting a little in the sun. Faint freckles accenting high cheekbones. And a mouth that he wanted to see smile. She looked absolutely perfect...except for the fact that the lower half of her dress was drenched. It made her look human. Vulnerable. Approachable.

And he found himself incapable of getting his bait and walking away. He wanted to spend time with her again. Felt like he simply *had* to. So he'd pretty much manipulated her into fishing with him this afternoon. It wasn't one of his finest moments. But he couldn't deny that he was looking forward to it.

They walked in comfortable silence toward the pond as if they did this all the time. And Ethan noted how simple this felt, how natural and…right. Spending an afternoon at this dazzling pond with a woman whom, regardless of his earnest attempts, he hadn't been able to get off his mind.

He heard chatter and looked away from Lindy to see the father-son duo heading out with their gear.

"Y'all going to give it a go?" the man asked.

"We are," Ethan said, lifting the rods and minnow bucket as he spoke. "How did y'all do?"

"We caught thirteen!" the little boy, who looked a little older than Jerry, said excitedly. "And guess what happened when I unhooked the last one?"

His father had already started shaking his

head. "Jordan, you don't need to tell them everything."

"He peed! I've never seen a fish do that before, have you?"

"Can't say that I have," Ethan said, and he heard Lindy's smothered laugh from beside him, while the man continued to shake his head.

"Boys will be boys," he said, but his easy smile and the way he ran a hand across the little guy's blond curls said he was loving spending the day with his son.

Ethan instantly pictured himself with Jerry one day, sharing funny, quirky conversations like this. "Yes," he said. "Boys will be boys."

Lindy's soft laughter halted, and Ethan glanced her way to see concern, or sadness, or a combination of the two etched on her features before she looked away from all of them.

But he hadn't misinterpreted that look.

What had just happened?

"We're heading home, Miss Lindy," the man continued, apparently unaware of the sudden change in her disposition. "Do you want me to put our rentals on the front porch?"

She turned to face them again, and Ethan noted her eyes glistening. "Yes," she said, seemingly gathering her composure. "That's fine."

The pair walked away, and Ethan and Lindy

resumed their pace, but now their silence was anything but comfortable. And after a moment that seemed as thick as the sorghum syrup the Tingles served him at breakfast this morning, Ethan said, "I'm sure it didn't hurt the fish."

Her expression faltered. "Wh-what?"

"It seemed like what Jordan said about the fish bothered you." But even as he made the statement, Ethan recalled hearing her laugh at the kid's exclamation. So if that wasn't it, then what had upset her?

Her grip tightened around the quilt she clutched against her chest. "That didn't bother me. I just…have a lot on my mind."

She'd made similar statements several times since they'd met. Ethan felt fairly certain that whatever was on her mind all the time had something to do with the past that had put her in a new town with no home, no job…and no family.

"Maybe some fishing will help you relax," he said.

She released her grip on the quilt and glanced out over the water sparkling in the afternoon sun. "I'm thinking if any place could help a person relax, this would be it."

"I'd have to agree," he said, glad that she seemed to be loosening up around the fishing hole. And around him. "What do you say we put the quilt down there?" He pointed toward the first big willow, its branches cascading so much that a few tips of the limbs dipped into the water with the breeze. "Based on what you said the other day about the fish liking the shade, that's where they're hiding, right?"

"Yes, they should be." She spread the quilt out beneath the willow. "But they will also hide in places that are out in full sun if it's tempting enough."

"Like where?" he asked.

"Like in a Christmas tree that's been submerged in the water." She tilted her head toward the pond. "Mr. and Mrs. Bowers have put a few out there, so that the fish aren't always at the bank, just in case some folks want to fish from one of the aluminum boats."

"Christmas trees? Seriously?" He scanned the water and wondered how many were hiding beneath the surface.

"Yes. You can put them in the water after Christmas, and it gives the fish a home. And if you mark the tree, like with a fishing bobber floating slightly beneath the surface, then you can find a good fishing spot throughout the year. That's the way Mr. and Mrs. Bowers mark theirs."

"That's amazing," he said, mesmerized as he watched her straighten the quilt. She moved around its perimeter, smoothing out the edges, her coral-tipped fingernails running along the border until the green, yellow and blue star-shaped design was perfectly centered.

She sat on the right side of that star but continued running her hand along the fabric as though enjoying the feel of the texture against her palm. "My grandmother and I would mark our spot with bobbers painted pink."

"You said she taught you how to fish, but it sounds like you fished a lot as a kid," he said, enjoying this glimpse into her youth. He wanted to know more, much more, about this interesting lady.

"We didn't have a lot of extra money growing up, so we would fish, and we'd eat whatever we caught for dinner," she said. "The best was crappie, and it's still my favorite. It's a white freshwater fish. Tastes like tilapia, if you like that."

"I do." He placed the minnow bucket and fishing rods beside the quilt, since he didn't want to accidentally spill any of the bait water on the fabric. Especially after Lindy had taken so much care with it.

In fact, she seemed to take particular care with everything. And she apparently enjoyed pretty, feminine things, like the dress she wore today, which was an interesting choice for spending the day working at a fishing hole and selling live bait. But it suited her, the Caribbean-blue fabric drawing attention to those vivid eyes. She'd paired the dress with sandals accented with tiny stones in beach hues of sea green, turquoise and coral. And her toenails were painted the same color as her fingernails.

"Ethan?" she asked.

"Yeah?"

"You're…staring."

Caught. He had no choice but to agree. But how was a guy supposed to be this close to her without staring? "Guilty as charged."

She seemed surprised by his admission, her eyes widening a little and her cheeks tingeing pink before her slender throat pulsed as she swallowed. "Why?"

"Why am I staring?"

She glanced down, her lashes fanning across her cheeks before she looked back up at him. "Yes, why?"

Because you're beautiful. Because you captivate me the way no woman has in a very long time. Because I've seen you with the little boy who's going to be mine, and I can tell how much you care about him. And because someone has hurt you, and I hate the thought of you being hurt. I don't want to think about you being hurt…ever.

"Because," he said, "I wouldn't think a woman would wear a dress to work at a fishing hole."

It was the truth, but it sure wasn't why he'd been staring.

"I wasn't able to wear dresses in p—" She paused, moistened her lips and then continued, "In my last position. And I got my first paycheck from Mr. and Mrs. Bowers yesterday, so I celebrated a little and bought this outfit from the consignment store in the square." She undid the tiny straps on her sandals, slipped them off and placed them beside her on the quilt. Then she looked at Ethan and added, "I probably didn't need to buy the shoes or the matching nail polish, but they were really good deals, and it's been a while since I got to shop for clothes."

Ethan didn't know why she felt the need to explain the purchase, but her questioning gaze made him want to reassure the fascinating lady. "I think it was a good purchase."

She looked down once more, then glanced up again, and he wished he could tell what was going on in her mind. "Thank you," she finally whispered. Then she cleared her throat. "We should probably get to fishing if you want to get some practice in before y'all come on Monday."

"Right," he said, following her lead and slipping off his shoes. It had felt good sitting out in the open fishing with Jerry on Wednesday, but here, sitting on the quilt under the willow tree with Lindy, their shoes off, it felt...nearly perfect.

Now, if they could just catch a fish.

He placed a minnow on the end of her hook and then handed her the fishing rod. "Ready to show me how this is done?"

"I don't know about that," she said, sliding the bobber up a little on her line before dropping the baited hook into the water. "But we'll see."

She sounded like she was enjoying herself, and Ethan was glad he was able to have some small part in that. Then, as he dropped his own bait in the water, her cork went beneath the surface.

"I got a bite!" She pulled up the line to display a shiny speckled fish on the end—at the same moment that Ethan's cork also headed south. "And you do, too. Pull it up!"

He yanked it up to see a similar, but smaller, fish on the end of his line. Laughing, he turned the pole so that their fishes dangled side by side. "We did it, didn't we?" The sense of accomplishment that welled through him at the sight of that tiny fish was ridiculous, but even so, indisputable. He'd actually caught a fish.

"Yes, we did," she said, and released the smile he'd waited to see. It reached her cheeks and, as he suspected, made her even more breathtaking.

It took him a moment to remember that this wasn't a date, or any type of romantic venture, because for the briefest second, he felt like pulling her close, hugging her, laughing with her, celebrating their catches…and kissing her.

Apparently, his thoughts had betrayed him, or maybe his attention had drifted to her mouth, because she ran her teeth over her lower lip and whispered, "Ethan?"

"Yeah?"

"We should probably…" She let the sentence hang.

He didn't know why she stopped, but he had to know the rest. "We should probably what, Lindy?"

She pulled her gaze away from him and turned her attention to the fish at the end of the line. "We should probably put the fish back in the water."

Chapter Seven

He'd wanted to kiss her.

Lindy had no doubt that he'd at least thought about it a moment ago. It'd been a long, long time since she'd experienced that feeling, the sensation of knowing a man wanted to kiss her, but she recognized it at once. And as much as she didn't want to admit it, she'd *wanted* to be kissed. By Ethan Green. The man whose primary goal was to take her son. She couldn't share anything remotely intimate with this man. He was the enemy.

However, as he baited her hook again and looked at her with those warm, chocolate eyes, a hint of a smile from their success still teasing the corners of his lips, she was finding it harder and harder to remember that fact.

Within another couple of minutes, her bobber went under, its red and white colors turning yellowish as it sunk beneath the wet surface. She pulled up the shimmering fish as Ethan's float jiggled with a nibble and then plummeted, as well.

She didn't wait for him to take her bream off the line, but removed it herself and gently tossed it back into the water.

Ethan unhooked his and did the same, his smile broadening with each passing moment. "Gotta admit, I've never really had a desire to fish, but this is pretty cool." He reached for the end of her line and put another minnow on without her asking.

The impulse to tell him she didn't need help was overshadowed by the need to express appreciation toward a guy who assisted a woman without being asked. "Thanks," she said.

"Thank *you* for helping me out today. I'm feeling a lot more optimistic about keeping my promise to Jerry now."

Lindy kept her focus on the red-and-white floater in the water, because she didn't want to look at him when she asked what she most wanted to know. She feared he'd see too much in her face. So she waited until they'd settled in peacefully to watch their corks in the water and let a little time pass.

After a few moments, and attempting to sound casual, she asked, "Why did you pick him? Why did you pick Jerry to adopt instead of another kid?"

Her hands tightened around the rod as she held her breath and waited to see what he'd say.

For a few seconds that seemed like an eternity, she worried he wouldn't answer. Then he released a thick breath and said, "I guess the main reason was…he reminded me of me at that age. And I just felt, I don't know, connected to him, even before we met, because of that." His cork bounced in the water, and he pulled up yet another fish that he easily unhooked and then tossed back into the pond. "That's three in less than a half hour," he said. "Not bad."

But Lindy wasn't done talking about Jerry yet. Her own bobber moved, and she suspected that her bait might be stolen by a hungry little fish soon, but she didn't care. She needed to learn more about the man who saw himself in her son.

Jerry didn't favor Ethan in looks at all. Her little boy had blond hair with a reddish hue. He had freckles and fair skin, much like hers. In contrast, Ethan had dark hair, skin that obviously didn't have a problem getting tan and not a freckle to be seen. Jerry had bright blue eyes. Ethan's were deep brown. So it wasn't Jerry's physical appearance that caused Ethan to relate to him.

Lindy suspected she knew what had triggered his interest in her child. Her attention moved to his leg, outstretched, and that wicked scar covering his right knee. She'd noticed a few other, less noticeable places on his skin, small puckers or discolorations. But that one looked like whatever had caused it had been very, very painful.

Odd, that the marred flesh didn't detract from his appeal. On the contrary, Lindy found herself even more impressed, even more attracted, to a male who had obviously been through something tough given those permanent reminders on his skin—perhaps even on his soul—and yet who seemed so at peace with his life.

She swallowed. If anything, it made him even more beautiful.

Lindy wanted to touch that scar, trace her fingers over the jagged lines and tell him that it didn't take away from the man that she was learning more about with each passing day.

A chill washed over her as she realized why her skin grew warm around him, why she couldn't stop thinking about him, why she wanted to find out how he'd been hurt.

She wanted a relationship with Ethan.

He'd busied himself with putting another minnow on his hook and placing it in the water.

But she couldn't stop looking at him and wondering what had happened in *his* past.

Finally, he glanced up and found her frowning, staring at his scar. "Ethan?"

He saw where her gaze had landed, but didn't say anything.

"What happened to you?" she asked, unable to control the concern in her tone—or the intense desire to somehow make his world better.

His mouth slid to the side, but then movement in the water caught his eye. "You've got one." He pointed to her cork, no longer visible.

Lindy had felt the telltale tug on the line, but she hadn't wanted to take her focus off finding out more about Ethan Green. However, now she had no choice, because he'd reached for the rod and yanked the fish out of the water.

"You nearly lost him," he said, giving her a different kind of smile, one that looked forced. After unhooking the fish, he tossed it in, where it slapped the water and then darted away.

Clearly, he didn't want to tell her anything about that scar. Or about his past. He reached toward the minnow bucket, but Lindy placed her hand on his forearm to stop his progress. She felt the warmth of his skin against her own, the slight brush of masculine hair against her palm. Her heart thundered in her chest. "Ethan, wait."

He released another thick breath before he turned and faced her. "Lindy," he said, his attention focused on her hand and, she now noticed, the small circular scar to the left of her thumb.

She moved her thumb slightly, so that the pad brushed across the puckered flesh. "What happened there?"

He hesitated and looked back toward his floater, still in the water and, thankfully, not moving.

"Please, Ethan. Tell me." She needed to know, even more than he realized. There was a reason he was so drawn to Jerry, and she thought she'd figured out why.

Again, she eased her thumb across the marred skin, slightly paler in color than the surrounding flesh. "Right here," she whispered. "What happened, Ethan?"

"That…was from a cigarette." While he spoke, she studied the slight imperfections more thoroughly. He was so beautiful, so masculine and seemingly perfect, all hard muscles and sturdy planes. But now that she looked closely, she saw so much more. A body that had been hurt.

A man who had been hurt.

Tiny lines crossed the top of each hand. Like he'd been cut a few times. There was more puckered skin from cigarette burns on his other forearm. At a distance, the lines and circles hadn't been as noticeable, except for the worst one, on his knee. But up close, and now that she truly looked, smaller scars were pretty much everywhere.

Oh, Ethan. Her heart squeezed tightly in her chest. "Were you— Did someone hurt you when you were Jerry's age? Is *that* why you feel connected to him?" It was too difficult to look away, and she wanted—needed—to see the emotion on his face. To know if his feelings were as real as she suspected.

"My father." He said it as though he had to push the words past his throat. "It took a few years, until I started school, before anyone noticed. Or rather, before anyone cared enough to say anything."

No wonder he'd felt a connection to Jerry.

She asked the obvious question. "What about your mother? Didn't she…?"

He shook his head emphatically before she could finish the question. "She stood by and let it happen. Often, she watched." His eyes closed slightly, as though picturing a scene from long ago. "Her hand would be over her mouth, as though she couldn't believe it was happening again. Every time. But she never said a word, never tried to stop him."

Lindy couldn't understand how any woman could stand by and allow her child to be harmed. But as quickly as she'd had the thought, the memory of that last night with Gil sliced fiercely through her mind. For the briefest moment, she *hadn't* been able to protect Jerry. And she'd never forgiven herself for that.

"How—how did you get him to finally stop?" she asked, remembering that last night, when she'd determined the only way to make Gil stop was to leave. She'd gathered her baby in her arms and ran, searching for the women's shelter, praying for her son's life. And her own.

The next morning, she'd been alive. So had Jerry. But Gil was dead. And she'd been charged with murder.

An icy chill moved through her with that painful memory.

"This." He indicated the horrific spiderlike scar on his right knee, which now seemed even worse when Lindy thought about how it must have gotten there—at his own father's hand. "*This* is how I got him to stop."

Lindy noticed how the scar wrapped around his knee completely.

"The night he did this, he'd gotten drunk and came home to find me asleep on the couch. I was supposed to sleep in my bed, but the television was in the living room, and I'd stayed up late to watch something on TV and fell asleep there. I tried to get up and make it to my room, but he caught me."

"He caught you." The vision playing in her mind was terrible. Ethan as a little boy, trying to get away from a grown man whose sole intent was to hurt his own son.

"Yeah…with a baseball bat."

Tears pushed free, and she brushed them away. "How old were you?"

"Six."

Six years old and facing a grown man, chasing him with a baseball bat. The one who should have been protecting him had scarred him for life instead. "No one helped you?"

"My first-grade teacher had reported that she suspected abuse, but no one had followed through, probably because my mother kept assuring them that I was fine."

"Couldn't you have told the teacher what was going on?" Lindy couldn't understand how the adults in Ethan's world hadn't protected him. Surely someone besides his first-grade teacher had noticed the cigarette burns. "Or didn't anyone else see anything and tell the authorities?"

He smiled, but there was nothing happy about it. "Long sleeves and blue jeans," he said. "Even in the summer, when it was ninety-plus degrees outside, my mother would have me wear long sleeves and blue jeans whenever we went out, so no one would see my scars. And if he'd done a number on my hands, which he sometimes did, she would simply keep me at home until they healed."

"You could have told someone, couldn't you?" She was having a tough time seeing how a little boy could have been so abused without anyone finding out.

"He had me so convinced that it'd get worse if I told anyone that I never said anything about what was really happening at home."

"What did your mother say about your injuries? Surely she had to explain why you were hurt so much."

"Oh, that was easy. She'd say that I had taken another fall outside, or down the stairs, or that I'd been trying to help her cook and cut myself, or burned myself. She was very believable." His voice dripped with admonition toward the woman who also should have protected him back then. "She didn't want him to hurt her, so she let him hurt me."

Lindy was astounded. How could any mother do that to her son? "Why—why would she do that?"

"She said that she loved him, no matter what he did. He'd tell her he was going to change, and she would believe him and stay. She *always* stayed." He pointed to the scarred knee. "And I guess I should be grateful for this, because it turns out that people no longer simply suspect that something is happening when the kid is beaten so bad that he can't stand up."

"What happened then, once everyone knew what was really going on at your house?"

"The state took custody and placed me in one of the group homes, and then I went into foster homes from that point on."

"You weren't adopted?"

An odd look, sadness combined with a hint of bitterness, passed over his face. "With the exception of babies, boys are tougher to place than girls," he said. "You'll hear that from every social worker around. And it's especially difficult if the kid is having a tough time dealing with his past or finds it hard to trust people. So I went through a lot of homes. And no, I wasn't ever adopted."

Her hand still rested on his forearm, and she squeezed it gently. "Ethan, I'm so sorry."

He gave her a grin laced with sadness. "Lindy, it was a long time ago, and I'm doing fine. It's just that, when I saw Jerry's story on the news and learned about his situation, that his daddy abused him and that his mother didn't do anything to stop it, it hit way too close to home. And I knew it was God's plan for me to help that little boy."

Lindy didn't know what to say. Now she knew why Ethan wanted her child, and she also wondered if he was right. What if it was God's plan for Ethan to adopt Jerry? If that was the case, then what chance did she have of getting custody of her son again?

And what court would tell Ethan no, when he shared his past and explained how very much he wanted to give Jerry the kind of life he never had?

Ethan leaned toward her, eased his shoulder against hers. "Hey, it's fine. Really. Don't look so sad. God and the army got me through the pain of my past. And I'm doing great now."

"The army?" Another surprise, and one that impressed her tremendously. He'd been abused by his parents, had spent the remainder of his youth in the foster system and had come out of it all doing well, with a great job and a desire to help another child.

And he'd served their country, too?

"Yeah," he answered. "When you turn eighteen and have no idea where to go, what to do, you look for a place to put a roof over your head and food in your belly. That's all I joined for, to be honest, but I got so much more. Learned so much more. About integrity and service and dedication. And then, after four years of deployment in Afghanistan, the army put me through college, and I achieved my first dream."

"Becoming a teacher?" she asked, even more amazed by this intriguing man. And feeling her heart pulled closer toward the guy she'd planned to loathe.

She was very, very far away from loathing now.

"Not becoming a teacher, necessarily, but becoming a mentor. I wanted to show kids that someone cared, just in case they weren't getting that at home. So teaching in a middle school, when they're going through those tough years, seemed like the best opportunity to accomplish that dream."

Everything about him impressed her. She wanted to ask him—beg him—to change his mind about adopting Jerry, because he could ruin her chances completely. But if she did that, he'd learn the truth about who she was, and she wasn't ready to divulge that secret yet. So instead, she said the second thing pricking her heart, prompted by her admiration for those who put their lives at risk for others. "Thank you for your service."

He placed his left hand on top of hers, which, she now realized, had never moved from his arm. His smile said he was used to gratitude. "Trust me, it was my pleasure. And you don't need to look so sad. I'm about to gain a son. And today, thanks to you, I learned to fish. My life has honestly never been better."

Lindy slid her hand free. "I'm glad for that," she said. And she meant it. She *was* glad that his life had gotten better, that he'd gotten over the pain of his abusive past. It gave her hope for Jerry to be happy and content again. But no matter how much she wanted to see Ethan happy after learning about his painful past, she didn't want all of his dreams to come true.

Because the dream she knew he wanted most would take her son away from her forever.

Ethan didn't know why he'd shared so much, but oddly, it hadn't bothered him as much as he'd have thought. He couldn't remember the last time he'd told anyone about his past. Even when he'd filled out the paperwork for the social worker, explaining why he wanted to adopt Jerry and how he could provide a good home for the boy, he hadn't felt the emotions, hadn't remembered the pain, so clearly. Maybe that'd been because the words had been written on paper rather than spoken.

Or maybe the difference was Lindy. There was something about her that made him want to open up, encouraged him to share the deepest parts of his past. He sensed a closeness with this exquisite woman that he hadn't felt in a very long time.

Since Jenny.

He needed to lighten the mood. And he needed to guard himself from letting this happen again. He didn't need to grow too close to Lindy. Very soon, hopefully, he'd adopt Jerry and move back to Birmingham. Lindy would presumably stay in Claremont. Or move somewhere else to run away from her own past. A past she hadn't shared with him yet.

And one he shouldn't ask about. That would only draw them closer, and he needed to keep that from happening. Nothing could come of this long-term, and he didn't want a relationship anyway. Not now. He was about to become a father for the first time. His concentration needed to be on his little man. Jerry deserved that.

So he'd turn this afternoon back into what it should be, two people becoming friends while sharing an afternoon fishing. Nothing more, nothing less.

He turned, scooped a minnow out of the bucket and then reached for her line. "We're wasting daylight, and I need all the practice fishing I can get."

Lindy watched him bait her hook. "So we're done talking about the past?"

He released the line, and she placed it in the water a short distance away from his cork, still floating. Ethan could've told her that he wanted to know about her past, as well. But she probably wouldn't share. And he shouldn't want to know. That would only bring them closer. And he felt close, way too close, already. "We're done talking about the past."

She nodded. "Okay."

She seemed fine not sharing her own past. Which made him wonder even more what she'd been through.

"My grandmother used to say that—that we were wasting daylight. But I haven't heard that phrase in a while. Where did you hear it?"

"Daddy Jim," he said. Even just the name was a good memory. "The last father figure I had while I was in the system. I moved in with him and his wife, Mama Reba, right before I turned seventeen. Stayed with them for that last year." He remembered how rebellious he'd been when he'd shown up on their little farm in south Alabama. He'd decided that no one wanted him, and so he wanted no one either. But Daddy Jim and Mama Reba had cared.

"What happened with them? Are they still in your life?"

"Actually, they are. In fact, I talked to them a few weeks ago, when I found out there was a chance that I could adopt Jerry. I need to call them and give them an update, in fact. They—well, I guess they'll have a grandson now after all, won't they?"

She glanced away, toward her cork in the water, but then she looked back at Ethan. "So everything wasn't always bad. You had some good memories?"

"I had good memories with them, and Daddy Jim was the one who talked to me about joining the army. He was retired military. I think they'd have probably adopted me if I'd have ended up at their place earlier, but I was pretty much an adult already by the time I got there. And they were both older."

She tilted her head, pushed a wayward strawberry tendril away from her face. "I bet, in their hearts, you're their son. They obviously love you."

She had no idea how much those words meant. He knew Daddy Jim and Mama Reba cared about him—they told him that all the time—but he'd never heard them express love. He'd kind of assumed that, maybe because of his military background, Daddy Jim considered himself too tough to express emotion. But that hadn't really bothered Ethan. He knew they cared.

He caught her gaze. She was still looking at him, waiting for a response he couldn't give, so he gave her a warning look and said, "I thought we were done talking about the past."

"But you had to answer my question about the wasting-daylight phrase. If you hadn't, that would've just been rude." She lifted a shoulder and smiled at him again. And it affected him as solidly as it had before.

Her cork went under, and she pulled up the line to show a fish on the end. "I'm ahead of you now. That's four for me."

Her grin was contagious. Glad she wasn't pressing the issue of foster parents, he returned the smile. "I'll catch up."

"That might be tough," she said as she removed her fish from the line and tossed it back in the pond.

"Why is that?"

"Because a hungry fish stole your bait while we were talking." She winked. "You didn't notice your cork go under? Disappeared completely."

He pulled up his line, and his hook was bare. "Why didn't you say anything?"

Another lift of the shoulder. "Because you

were talking, and I wanted to hear what you had to say."

He laughed, an honest-to-goodness laugh, and realized he hadn't enjoyed an afternoon this much in quite some time. "You're really something, Lindy Burnett. I'm wondering if I shouldn't be a bit afraid of you."

She turned her attention toward the minnow he'd placed on the end of her line. "Maybe," she said. "Maybe you should be."

Chapter Eight

Ethan knocked on the door of the store at the fishing hole at seven thirty Monday morning and called Lindy's name upon entering. The last thing he wanted to do was startle her again, but he needn't worry; the place was empty. He'd seen her car parked outside, though, so he knew she was here somewhere. "Lindy?" he called, moving toward the back, where the tempting scent of fresh coffee filled the air. He'd already had one cup at the B and B, but he could stand to have another. He'd wait though. First things first. He wanted—needed—to see her.

Extra quilts were stacked at one side of the back entrance that led to the deck, and an old-fashioned galvanized tub filled with ice and water bottles held fort on the opposite side. Ethan felt a twinge of guilt for not showing up earlier like he'd intended. He could've helped her carry in the quilts or ice down the water.

Then again, she was doing all of those things on her own each morning. It wasn't like she needed any help with her job.

But Ethan *wanted* to help her in any way, even with something as trivial as icing down water bottles. Based on the few things he'd learned about Lindy Burnett, it seemed she hadn't received a lot of help in life. And he felt the impulse to show her that someone, somewhere, cared.

Because he did.

Thinking he'd probably find her outside, he stepped onto the deck, scanned the pond and noticed a thin coating of fog hovering above the surface.

Then he saw her, walking along the water's edge.

For a moment, all he could do was stare. The morning sky was overcast, except for one small circular break in the clouds, and yellow rays of sunlight streamed through, illuminating the woman by the pond. Her beauty had his breath catching in his throat.

Long strawberry curls tumbled freely and moved slightly as she walked. One hand rested against her throat, the way it often did when she was thinking, or when she was troubled.

Odd, that he'd spent so little time with her yet already knew her mannerisms well enough to know when she was anxious. Or worried.

Was there anything he could do to calm her fears?

He shook his head, perturbed that he was heading down *that* path again, the one that had caused him to fall for Jenny—and the one that had pretty much shattered his heart in the process.

Wearing a long, pale yellow dress that made her appear even more feminine, even more vulnerable, she took her time as she eased along the mossy bank. Occasionally, she would pause and bow her head slightly.

Was she praying? She'd been at church yesterday, and he'd visited with her for a few moments afterward when he was seeing Jerry off to the bus. She'd talked to the two of them and asked his future son if she could give him a hug. Jerry had obliged, even smiled as he told her goodbye. And Ethan had felt a tug deep inside at how she obviously cared about the little boy—probably because Ethan had shared more of Jerry's story with her on Saturday—and also how much Jerry cared about her.

But after the Willow's Haven bus had left the church parking lot, Ethan had turned to find that she'd gone. Driven away without even saying goodbye.

He'd felt certain they'd shared a special moment, or a few of them, on Saturday. Yet she'd driven away without looking back.

And Ethan hadn't stopped thinking about her ever since.

Who was he kidding? He hadn't stopped thinking about her since they'd first met that day at the fountain.

A fish jumped in the water, and she looked toward the ripple in the surface, which caused her to pivot…and see Ethan.

Smile, Lindy.

He wanted to see some acknowledgment that they had shared something special two days ago. He lifted a hand and, after a brief hesitation, she responded, the hand at her throat moving ever so slightly.

Ethan *hadn't* imagined the connection they'd experienced Saturday beneath that willow tree. He replayed that entrancing moment when she'd touched his scar, tenderly run her fingers across the jagged lines and looked at him as though she wished she could take the pain of the past away.

She might as well have placed those compassionate fingers on his heart, because *that* was where she'd touched him the most.

He found himself counting the seconds until she reached the back deck. He wanted to see her, talk to her, simply be around her. "I thought I'd come early and help you set up," he said as she finally drew near.

Her eyes lifted, then her cheeks followed suit and a subtle smile played at the corners of her mouth. "A little late for that, aren't you?" Her tone was close to teasing, definitely near flirtatious.

Was she flirting?

And shouldn't that sound warning bells within him, instead of firing off some sort of inexplicable excitement?

"I'd planned to come earlier, but I had promised Mrs. Tingle I would try her new apple puff pastry. She wants to put it on the B and B menu as a regular item, but needed a guinea pig for the tasting."

"And you were the chosen guinea pig?" That flicker of a smile was still there.

"I'm the only one staying at the bed-and-breakfast long-term, so yeah, I'm the current resident guinea pig." He held up the bag holding the to-go box he'd carried from the B and B. "But when it involves trying things like this, I'll be a guinea pig any day of the week."

"You brought some with you?" Her hand moved to her throat, and he saw that she touched a tiny gold cross suspended from a thin chain. "You must have really liked it."

"Not for me." He extended the box toward her. "It's amazing, and I thought you might like to try it."

Her eyes softened but she looked more confused than surprised. Then she visibly swallowed and asked, "You brought *me* some?"

Her question was filled with emotion, and oddly enough, Ethan detected more sadness than pleasure. She was genuinely touched by the simple gift of an apple puff pastry. Ethan wasn't sure how to respond. Had no one ever done anything like that for her before? And if not, why?

He attempted to lighten the mood and laughed. "Don't tell me you're allergic to apples."

She shook her head. Blinked. Swallowed. Blinked again. "You're…going to make this difficult," she whispered.

Ethan had no idea what she meant. "Make what difficult?"

Her hand tugged at the tiny cross, and she gave him a forced smile. "Not eating sweets this early," she answered.

Ethan had no doubt that wasn't what she was really referring to, but he wasn't going to press the issue. "So you don't want to try it?" He waved it near her nose.

"I can smell the cinnamon and the apples, and I think the butter, too." She inhaled deeply. "If it tastes as good as it smells…"

"Trust me, it does." He opened the bag and withdrew the box, the clear lid displaying the puff pastry surrounding the warm apple filling. "You know you want to try it."

"I can't remember the last time I've had anything that smelled that good—and yes, I do want to try it."

He was glad to see that she'd let her guard down a little, her blue eyes lighting up the way they had Saturday when they'd been catching those fish.

Her stomach growled loudly, and she moved her hand from her throat to her waist. "I— didn't get a chance to eat breakfast. I'd planned on getting some fruit or a granola bar from the store once I checked in all the kids and mentors this morning."

Ethan glanced at his watch. "We still have fifteen minutes before they get here. You might as well give this a try while it's still warm instead of waiting until after they check in."

"It's still warm?" Her stomach growled again.

Ethan grinned. "Absolutely, and it sounds like you need it." He moved toward a small wrought iron table and chairs and placed the box in front of one of the chairs, along with the utensils Mrs. Tingle had packed. "I didn't think to bring you anything to drink. But I saw the coffee inside. I'll get you a cup."

"I can get it," she said, starting toward the door.

Ethan caught her hand as she started to pass. "Because I ran later than I intended, you don't have a lot of time to enjoy this. So you sit here and get started, and I'll fix your coffee. What do you take in it?"

Her skin was so fair that he easily noticed her blush. "You don't need to do that, Ethan," she said, attempting to ease her arm from his hand.

Instead of releasing her, he placed his hand at the small of her back and gently guided her to the table. "I know I don't need to. I want to."

She complied and sat in the chair, then picked up the utensils. "You're used to getting your way, aren't you?"

He shook his head. "Nah, not really. I'm just determined to make sure you enjoy your breakfast. So what do you take in your coffee?"

She let out a resigned sigh. "Cream and two sugars, please."

"Consider it done. And don't wait for the coffee to try the pastry."

She'd already pushed the fork into the warm apple center. "I couldn't wait if I tried."

Before Ethan entered the store, he saw her take the first bite. She looked like a child who'd discovered ice cream, her eyes closing as she chewed, mouth curving into a smile and throat emitting a contented hum as she swallowed. "Wow," she exclaimed softly.

Ethan would've brought a whole box of pastries if he'd have known he'd get that kind of response. Pleased with himself, he went inside and headed for the coffee counter. There, he selected a turquoise coffee mug with yellow daisies hand-painted around the edge, filled it with coffee, then added cream and sugar, before grabbing a second mug, this one plain brown, and filling it with black coffee for himself.

By the time he returned to the deck, she'd eaten three-fourths of the pastry.

"I must have taken too long fixing the coffee," he said, placing the steaming blue mug on the table near what remained of her breakfast.

A soft laugh escaped. "You didn't take too long," she said. "I'm pretty sure I've been inhaling this thing. It's just so good." She took another small bite, placed her fork on the plate and reached for the mug. Wrapping her hands around it, she blew a steady stream of air across the top of the liquid and then took a sip. "Mmm."

Even the way she drank her coffee showed appreciation and gratitude. It sure didn't take much to impress her.

"That good, huh?" he asked.

She glanced up, and he noticed the confusion still in her eyes, which were glistening with what appeared to be unshed tears. "Ethan?"

He really liked the way she said his name. "Yeah?"

"I...can't remember the last time anyone has ever done anything like this for me. And I, well, I want you to know how much I appreciate it." She moistened her lips, and Ethan's attention moved there, his mind acknowledging that he really wanted to kiss this beautiful lady.

Reeling it in, he reminded himself of the mistakes of his past. Trusting too soon, getting hurt too fast. He took a sip of his coffee, letting the strong, hot liquid jolt him back to his senses. He didn't need to get too close. "That's just what guys do," he said.

She took another sip. "Not all guys." Her words were spoken so softly that he almost didn't hear. But he did. And with them, he got another small glimpse into the pain of her past.

He didn't know who had hurt her, whether it was a family member or a friend or a guy. But now he knew. And he had a very sudden impulse to hurt the man who'd hurt Lindy Burnett.

She exhaled thickly. "I ate way too much."

He knew better than to bring the subject back to her past. It would undoubtedly start a lengthy conversation, and the kids would be here soon. Plus, he wasn't certain he could handle hearing about her past without wanting to fix things. So he tapped a finger against the table near the pastry box. "You don't have that much left," he said. "You can do it."

She pushed the box toward him and held up her palms in surrender. "No, I can't. I'm done. Spent. I'll probably need a nap when this sugar wears off."

"All right then." He laughed and took her remnants to the trash can nearby.

"You didn't need to clean up for me," she said. "It's enough that you brought me breakfast and fixed my coffee."

"Like I said, this is just what I do." He intentionally changed up the phrasing a bit, since she'd already hinted that not all guys treated a lady with respect. Even though they should.

"Lindy?" Mrs. Bowers stood at the bottom step at the opposite end of the deck.

Ethan wondered how long she'd been there, and whether she'd heard any of their conversation.

"Mrs. Bowers." Lindy got up from the table and nervously ran her palms along the sides of her dress as she stood. "I've got everything ready for the Willow's Haven group."

The woman climbed the steps, and Ethan noticed her eyes soften toward Lindy, and then slowly move from Lindy to Ethan and back again. "I know you have everything ready," she said. "You're doing a great job out here, Lindy. I've had several people say so already, and it doesn't surprise me. God sent you here, I'm sure of it."

Lindy's features visibly relaxed. Ethan assumed she had been fearful of a reprimand for sitting down on the job, but surely visiting with guests was part of what Mrs. Bowers expected, and from the look on her face, she was anything but disappointed in her newest employee. Besides, this guest had technically arrived before the workday had officially begun.

Sure enough, Mrs. Bowers said, "You've been doing such a good job, Lindy, that James and I want to give you a paid vacation day."

Lindy's eyes widened. "A paid vacation day? I've only been working here a week."

"So we'll consider it your one-week reward."

Mrs. Bowers clapped her hands together and grinned broadly. "Doesn't that sound great?"

Lindy blinked and nodded. "Yes, ma'am, it does."

Mrs. Bowers beamed. "Wonderful," she said, then held a finger in the air. "Oh, but there's one little catch."

"What's that?" Lindy asked.

"You have to take it this Friday."

Ethan had never heard of anything this bizarre, giving a paid vacation day after a week of work—and then requiring it to be taken on a certain day—but the enthusiasm in the tiny woman's tone and the way she was practically bouncing on her heels with excitement had him grinning. It was good to see someone going out of their way to be nice to Lindy, particularly since she apparently hadn't had a lot of people be kind to her in the past. "Sounds like a good deal to me," he said.

"This Friday," Lindy repeated, clearly baffled.

"That's right," Mrs. Bowers said. She pivoted from one foot to the other then placed her finger against her cheek. "Oh, and come to think of it, I have the perfect idea for what you should do on your day off."

"What I should do?" Lindy asked as the low rumble of the school bus echoed in the distance.

"Savvy told me that the kids from the children's home were going to the zoo in Stockville on Friday. I've seen how much you enjoy interacting with the kids and thought you might like to go along and help her with the chaperoning, if you don't mind."

Lindy's mouth opened, her eyes sparkled and she immediately started nodding. "Oh, yes, Mrs. Bowers, yes. I'd like that very much."

The woman clapped her hands together again. "Perfect! I'll let Savvy know she can count on you as another chaperone." Then she turned to Ethan. "And Savvy said that you'll be going, too? With Jerry?"

"I will," Ethan said, even more excited for the day now that Lindy would be there, too.

"Well, isn't that wonderful," Mrs. Bowers said, as the bus's brakes squeaked loudly from the parking lot.

"I'm going inside to get ready to check the kids in," Lindy said. "Thank you for the paid day off, Mrs. Bowers. I really appreciate it, and I know I'll enjoy spending the day with the kids." She darted through the back door, and Ethan heard her call out to some of the older teens who had already hurried inside, anxious to get their gear.

Ethan started to follow after her, but a tap

on his biceps caused him to turn toward Mrs. Bowers. She had one eyebrow lifted.

"There's something you don't know about me," she said.

Ethan knew hardly anything about her, other than that she seemed amazingly sweet, she loved God and she'd been kind—very kind— to Lindy. But he had a feeling none of those things were what she was referring to. So he asked, "What's that?"

"My grandson, Troy, used to work here at the fishing hole. Until I introduced him to Destiny, who he's now married to." She nodded and smiled. "He couldn't work here anymore, because Destiny is a big-time author, and they're on a book tour now."

"That's…great," he said, unsure why this was something he needed to know.

"Yep, it is." She placed one hand on her hip and flipped the other palm in the air as she continued, "And then there's Brodie and Savvy. She'd really been miffed at the fellow for a mistake he made in the past. It was a bad decision on his part, but you know, everyone makes mistakes, now, don't they?"

Ethan was trying to keep up with her train of thought. "Yes, ma'am, they do."

She clicked her tongue against the roof of her mouth and shook her head. "It took a little work, but I got her to come around and realize that boy had been forgiven by God and that he should be forgiven by her too. And I just knew God had planned for her to be with him. Now look at them, running such a wonderful children's home and helping to give those kids another chance at family."

"That's…great, too," he said, and suddenly thought he knew where this conversation was headed.

"There's a few more I could tell you about, but we don't have a lot of time—I'm sure you're ready to go see your little boy. But I just wanted to let you know, about that paid day off I gave Lindy on Friday…"

"Yes, ma'am."

"I was pretty much giving that to you, too." She poked his biceps a little harder. "So don't waste it." Then she winked, turned on her heel and headed inside to help Lindy with the kids.

Ethan laughed, thinking this town—and the people in it—became more and more interesting by the minute. Even though he and Jerry would be moving to Birmingham as soon as the adoption was finalized, he could see himself coming here every summer, spending his vacation with the folks he'd already come to care about so much and maybe even doing some volunteer work with Willow's Haven. Sure, he wanted to help Jerry have a real family, but—thinking back to the loneliest years of his own childhood—he knew the other kids could use plenty of folks to show them they were loved.

Thinking of those kids, and the one he'd adopt soon, he entered the store to see the Willow's Haven crew getting bait, fishing rods and love from Lindy, Mrs. Bowers, Savvy and the mentors.

He scanned the group and finally spotted his little guy standing beside Savvy. "Hey there, Jerry. Are you ready to try to catch a fish today?"

Jerry looked happy to see Ethan, which was good, but the look quickly converted into a hint of skepticism. "Do you think we *can*?"

Savvy, still standing beside him, leaned over and gave his small shoulders a squeeze. "Of course you can," she answered.

Ethan said, "Tell you what, we're going to give it our best shot."

Jerry looked to Savvy. "We didn't catch anything last time. Not even one. They were playing hide-and-seek with us."

Savvy held her grin in check. "Then maybe today will be your day," she said consolingly.

"Maybe it will," Ethan agreed. "And do you know why I think it *will* be our day?"

Jerry's blue eyes lifted, freckles shifting on his cheeks. "No, why?"

"Because I've been practicing, and I've learned a few things about where those fish hide, thanks to Miss Lindy. She taught me how to find them, so we'll be better at the seeking part this time."

Lindy stood handing out fishing rods and bait a few feet away, but at the sound of her name, she turned to them.

"Miss Lindy, did you really teach Mr. Ethan about where the fish hide?" Jerry asked, more than a hint of awe in his tone.

Lindy handed a Styrofoam bucket of minnows to one of the mentors and lowered herself to eye level with Jerry. "I did my best to teach him," she said, and grinned up at Ethan. "You can tell me if he remembered the lesson after y'all get done today."

"How will I know?" Jerry asked.

She smiled, an honest-to-goodness, all-the-way-to-her-eyes kind of smile, and Ethan's heart tripped in his chest. "You'll know because—" she touched the tip of Jerry's nose "—if he remembers where they're hiding, you'll catch some fish."

"*Some* fish? Like maybe lots of them?" he asked hopefully.

"That's what I'm counting on," she said.

"How many do you think I'll catch?"

"Hmm," she said, clearly enjoying this conversation. "I'm gonna say…you'll catch nine."

Jerry squinted, thinking. "I'm guessing… eleventeen."

Lindy ruffled his hair. "Eleventeen, huh? Now, that's a lot of fish," she said, without cracking even a hint of a grin. She held out her palm. "High five?"

Jerry smacked his hand to hers and grinned. Then he looked up at Ethan. "We're going to catch a bunch if you can remember what Miss Lindy taught you. Aren't we?"

"We're sure going to try," Ethan said, tossing another prayer toward heaven that God would find it in His heart to put a few fish on the end of their lines today.

"Bye, Miss Lindy," Jerry said.

"Come see me and tell me all about your fish before you leave today, okay?" she asked.

"Okay," he agreed.

"Let's head out to the pond," Ethan said, "and I'll show you that hiding place."

"Okay!" Jerry started toward the door, but Ethan waited a beat to speak to Lindy.

"Thank you for helping me get ready for this. I've been praying we catch a few for him. He's really started coming out of his shell, opening up and seeming happy. I can't wait for Candace to see how well everything's going on Friday."

"Candace?" she asked. "The social worker is coming Friday?"

"To the zoo with us, so she can log our progress for the court." He looked toward Jerry, chatting with another child on the front porch. "She said that he's always started coming out of his shell in every placement, but then he withdraws again when he's placed in another home. This time, though, he'll be staying for good. So maybe this happy little guy I'm getting to know will remain happy for good." He winked. "*That's* what I'm hoping she sees on Friday."

"I'm glad I'll be there Friday," she said softly.

"I am, too," he said, and he thought he'd do his best to follow Mrs. Bowers's advice while they were at the zoo, and not waste the day.

It took Lindy almost an hour to check in all the kids and mentors and provide them with everything they needed for an enjoyable day at the pond. Most picked up quilts, bait and rental equipment, unless they had brought their own equipment, like Ethan. Some purchased sunscreen, and she was glad that Ethan had bought some for him and her fair-skinned son, even though the majority of their day would be in the shade.

From the back deck, she watched them, sitting in the very same spot where she had fished with Ethan on Saturday. And where Ethan had claimed a little piece of her heart.

He was just so perfect.

Okay, she knew no one was *perfect*, and she also remembered how Gil could appear that way in public and be the complete opposite in private, but still…she couldn't stop thinking that maybe, just maybe, Ethan Green was the real deal.

And if he was, or even if he was so good at pretending that a court would believe him, there was a very real possibility that she would lose any chance of having Jerry in her life again.

Lindy glanced back into the store to make sure there weren't any late stragglers needing equipment or bait. As she suspected, it was empty. Everyone had headed to the water to start fishing. They were all a little more eager today, because the forecast called for rain, and there was already a thick cover of clouds. Everyone wanted to get their time in before the storm hit. Lindy watched the sky's hue shift in ominous shades of gray.

She honestly didn't want to hurt Ethan. He'd been through so much, and he sure seemed to care about Jerry and what was best for him.

But Lindy did, too.

She withdrew her cell phone from the pocket of her dress and saw that it was after nine. She'd been waiting to make this call ever since Ethan left the fishing hole Saturday, but now her attorney's office was finally open.

She dialed the number, waited for the receptionist to connect her with the man set to plead her case and then explained why she felt like Ethan would win, if a court met both of them and had to choose.

"So I wanted to see if you could have a court determine whether I can have custody again without considering the person who wants to adopt Jerry now." She'd been rehearsing this nonstop, and she barged ahead. "Because Jerry was wrongfully taken from me. They thought I was guilty, but I wasn't, and that's been proved now. And Jerry hasn't been adopted yet. Can't we try to get my rights back, and get my little boy back, without factoring in the person who wants to adopt him now?"

She watched Jerry and Ethan in the distance while she waited for Ted Murrell's response. Ethan said something and gently shoved against Jerry, then pointed toward their bobbers in the water. Jerry looked up at Ethan and appeared to be laughing.

Laughing.

Her stomach pitched. What was she doing?

"The court has already been notified by the state about the status of the pending adoption," her attorney explained. "They *have* to be made aware of Jerry's current situation as part of the evaluation process. I don't see any way that he or she won't ask to meet the potential parent."

Lindy wanted to cry. If any court pitted her against Ethan Green, she'd lose her son.

"But," the man continued, "as I've mentioned before, the fact that the adoption hasn't gone through yet will prove to be in our favor. However…"

"However?" she questioned, still watching her little boy bond with a man who could turn out to be his daddy if she didn't convince this attorney, and then a judge, to give her parental rights back.

"However, a lot would depend on the judge assigned to our case. If we get a judge who is known for family reunification at any cost, then we should receive a decision in your favor. But if we get a judge who is known for situational ruling, that is, a ruling based on the child's current situation, and if this man is as good as you have described…"

She watched Jerry and Ethan, who appeared to both be laughing now, in the distance. "He is," she said, "or rather, he sure appears to be."

"Then," Mr. Murrell continued, "if our judge

rules based on the current situation, then I would wager that the odds would not be in our favor."

Lindy swallowed past the sudden thick lump in her throat. "In other words, whether or not I will have Jerry in my life again depends on the judge we receive."

"Most likely, yes. And the adoption not going through. If the adoption goes through while we're waiting to get in, we'll be bringing a reverse adoption to court, and that'll make it tougher to get a ruling in our favor, because legally Jerry will be his son."

She had to do something. She couldn't merely stand by and let someone, even Ethan, take her child away for good. "What is my best chance to get Jerry back? What can we do to get a judge who wants families reunited?"

"Your best chance would be to get in front of a judge before that adoption goes through. And I might have a way to make that happen, but it doesn't come without risk."

"What would you do?" she asked, watching the thick storm clouds churning overhead.

"I can put in a request to expedite the decision based on the fact that you've already been unjustly separated from your child for three years. That should prompt the state to move the case to the next docket."

A glimmer of hope spread through her. "So we could get a decision quicker." Before Ethan had even more time to bond with Jerry and therefore find it easier to convince a court that Jerry should be with him. "Yes, let's do that," she said, and then remembered his caveat. "But why would that be risky?"

"Because it will limit your time to reestablish yourself in society, show that you can provide a good home for Jerry, that you can keep a job and that you can bond with your child."

He paused, while Lindy processed this. She'd only been working for a week. She was living rent-free above the sporting goods store. And she hadn't had a whole lot of time with Jerry to allow for any bonding.

A hefty cough echoed through the line. "Those are things that any judge will evaluate. So, do you want me to expedite the case, Ms. Burnett?" he asked.

She peered toward that willow tree where she'd shared an amazing day with Ethan, watching as Jerry yanked on his fishing pole and found a small fish on the end of the line. He jumped up and raised the pole above his head, while Ethan clapped and then punched both hands in the air in victory.

Ethan Green just had a "first" moment with her son. Jerry had caught his first fish with

Ethan. Lindy had been there the first time he'd rolled over. The first time he'd sat up on his own. When he'd taken his first steps. And when he'd said "mama" for the very first time.

How she'd love to hear him say that again.

But now Ethan was stealing *her* firsts. And no matter how much she cared for the man, those moments were meant to be hers.

"Yes," she said. "Please expedite it. I want to go to court. As soon as possible."

Chapter Nine

Ethan watched Jerry and Lindy board the train at the zoo while he sat with Candace to learn more details about the unexpected developments in his case. They'd been touring the zoo with the Willow's Haven kids all morning, but Candace had wanted a chance to speak privately with Ethan, and Lindy had offered to take Jerry on the train so they could talk.

He was very grateful, and judging from the smiles and enthusiastic waves as the train passed near the picnic table where he and Candace sat, that was A-OK with Jerry, too.

"He's doing remarkably well, better than we've seen at any of his previous placements," Candace said, typing on her laptop as she spoke. "And even though he hasn't been placed with you yet, the fact that he's so undeniably content around you should prove to be an advantage when we meet with the judge."

"He still has some quiet moments," Ethan admitted. "And sometimes he looks sad." It hadn't happened as much since that very first day fishing, but every now and then, the child's attention drifted and his smile wavered, and Ethan feared it was the pain of his past creeping in.

Candace stopped typing and gave him a soft smile. "No child is happy 24/7, Ethan, and Jerry will be no exception. As a parent, it isn't your job to make sure he's happy all the time. It's your job to care for him, love him, protect him and teach him. Sometimes that will involve saying no, and most children don't want to hear that from anyone. But that doesn't mean he isn't happy overall and that you aren't doing what's best for your child."

"That's good to know," Ethan said. He was still bothered anytime Jerry was quieter than usual. However, that wasn't happening nearly as often lately. Then again, the majority of their time together was spent doing things most any kid would enjoy—fishing, going to the zoo...

"You're going to do just fine," she said. "I'm sure the court will agree, and I also think the court will agree that Jerry's birth mother shouldn't be trusted to take care of her child now, since she didn't protect him as an infant."

"I'm still surprised that she asked for the case to be expedited," he said. It certainly hadn't been what he'd expected to hear from the social worker, but that'd been the first thing she'd told him today.

"It was a bold, and perhaps clever, move on her attorney's part. But it's also risky, and truthfully, I'm a little shocked the woman is taking that kind of chance with custody of her son."

A group of Willow's Haven kids headed toward their table on their way to the lion exhibit a short distance away. A loud roar from that direction caused several of the girls to squeal and wrap their arms around each other, while the boys cheered. Then they all started practically running to the huge rock entrance to the Lion's Den.

"Hey, Mr. Green!" Dylan Evans called, following the little ones toward the exhibit. "Where's Jerr-Bear?"

"Hey, Dylan," Ethan answered. "He's riding the train with Lindy."

"Cool," the boy said. "When he gets back, if he wants to see the lions, I can take him. I told all the little kids I'd take them, and I don't want to let him down."

"Thanks," Ethan said. "I had planned on taking him there next, but I'm sure he'd like going with a 'big kid' like you."

Dylan laughed. "Sounds good. See ya later, Mr. Green."

"See you later, Dylan." Ethan watched the teen lead a large group of the little ones beyond that massive rock entrance, and he wondered if Jerry would be a leader like that one day. Would he be that friendly? That eager to help others?

Ethan suspected he would, because Ethan would teach him to be that way. They'd spend time together, learn about life together and, more important, learn about God together. Dylan Evans was obviously a good kid. Ethan had every intention of making sure Jerry became a good kid too.

He couldn't wait. And since Jerry's mother had asked to expedite the case, he wouldn't have to wait long.

"Why was it risky for her to move the case up?" he asked Candace.

"Because the decision will totally depend on the judge we draw. If we get a judge who is hands-down a family reunification judge, she'll win. But if the judge truly cares about the well-being of the child, there will be no contest. Jerry *will* be your son." She tapped fiercely on her laptop.

"He'll be my son," Ethan repeated, enjoying the thought of taking him back to Birmingham and showing him his room, which Ethan had already decorated in a baseball theme before he came to Claremont. He smiled. More than likely, he'd be swapping it out for fishing decor once he returned home.

Well, it turned out he enjoyed fishing, too, especially with his son.

"Yes, he will be your son," Candace said with a confident smile. "And I'm working on his case file, which will detail how well he's doing with you and how I can wholeheartedly recommend you as his legal parent. I'll also recommend for the adoption to go through as soon as possible."

"Do you think our chances of getting a judge who will rule for us are good?"

"There are a few judges who rule for family reunification at all costs. But from what I've seen in most recent cases, the majority of the courts thankfully lean toward what's best for the child," she said, still typing fiercely, "and this report will definitely identify you as the best parent for Jerry."

"I can't tell you how much I appreciate your help," Ethan said as the red wooden train completed its path around the zoo's perimeter and pulled back into the station.

He scanned the adults and kids onboard until he spotted the attractive woman in the big, floppy straw hat, long green jersey dress and sandals. She'd taken his breath away when he'd first seen her this morning, but he'd become used to the fact that the vision of Lindy Burnett had that effect on him.

Lindy pointed toward a peacock casually walking along the sidewalk near the train. It spread its feathers proudly. She said something to Jerry, who held both arms up as though displaying his own "feathers."

Candace tapped a few more keys and then closed the laptop. "Okay. The report is done, but I'll read over it again when I get back to the office before sending it in. If I've done my job right, there shouldn't be any question about who should have custody of Jerry Flinn."

"Can't wait until he's Jerry Green," Ethan said, still watching Lindy and Jerry.

"You and me both." Candace followed his gaze to the pair across the path. Lindy had gotten off the train first and held her arms out for Jerry to jump into them. Jerry, giggling, hurled himself wholeheartedly toward her, causing her to take a step backward, losing her footing on the pebbled rocks on the edge of the track.

Ethan moved, but there was no way he could make it to catch her before she fell, and he watched them tumble to the ground. "Oh, no." He stood, but they were already sitting up on the soft earth near the train tracks, Lindy quickly checking Jerry over, and then his laughter—and hers—drifted through the air. Both laughed so hard they had to hold their stomachs.

Something shifted inside Ethan, a happiness even stronger than what he felt around his future son. Hearing Jerry laugh touched his heart, but adding that laugh to Lindy's made his joy topple over. Grinning, he sat back down and found Candace also smiling at the display... and at him.

"Jerry really likes her, doesn't he?" she asked.

"Yes, he does," Ethan said. *And as much as I've attempted to fight it, so do I.*

"Is she doing better now? She seemed so sad that day when I first met her, but she looks much better now. I take it the job at the sporting goods store is working well for her?"

"She seems to love it," Ethan said. "And she's good at it, especially since Mr. and Mrs. Bowers have her working with the kids from Willow's Haven in their fishing program. She's obviously great with children."

Candace nodded, watching Lindy get up from the ground and, still laughing, extend a hand toward Jerry. "She mentioned wanting to adopt. I'll need to talk to her about that. I sense she'd probably make a great mother to a child."

Ethan couldn't disagree.

"You know, that's one thing that would have improved your chances, but it isn't as big of a factor nowadays as it was, say, fifteen years ago."

"What's that?" he asked.

"A two-parent family," she said. "When I first started in social work, it was almost impossible to get an adoption to go through for a single parent. Now it's definitely possible, though almost every judge would prefer to place a child in a two-parent home." She nodded toward Lindy and Jerry. "But thankfully, with modern society such as it is, the courts often have no choice but to place children in single-parent homes, which gives great opportunities to people like you, and Lindy."

Ethan had almost forgotten about Lindy's comment that first day, that she wanted to adopt a child but didn't feel she had anything to offer a little boy or girl. Now, after spending time with her, and particularly after seeing the way she interacted with Jerry and all of the other Willow's Haven children, Ethan had no doubt that a kid would be blessed to have a mother like her.

And, though he certainly wasn't going to admit it or act on it, a man would be blessed to have a wife like her, too.

* * *

Lindy couldn't imagine a better gift than the one Mr. and Mrs. Bowers had given her, a paid day off to spend with her son. Jerry was so excited about everything at the zoo, and she relished his exuberance during their train ride together. Even though they had seen a good portion of the exhibits this morning, he'd spotted several more animals he wanted to visit before the day ended, and Lindy wanted to make sure he got to see each and every one. He'd never been to a zoo before, and his enthusiasm was contagious. She almost felt like this was *her* first trip, too, as she saw it all through her son's eyes.

It was so delightful to experience this "first" with her little boy. She'd had a difficult time watching Ethan have his "first" with Jerry the other day when the two of them were fishing, but she thanked God that, even though Ethan was a part of this memory, too, she'd also been included in Jerry's first zoo trip.

"What are those pink birds called, Miss Lindy?" He pointed to the large pond in the center of the zoo, where several salmon-colored flamingos mingled along one edge.

"Those are flamingos."

"I like them, but pink is a girl color. Micah said so."

"Who's Micah?" she asked, enjoying learning more about his world. She imagined picking him up from school each afternoon and asking him all about his day. "Is that one of your friends?"

"He was, but I won't get to see him anymore." Jerry tried balancing on one leg like the flamingos, lost his balance and grabbed her hand. "Whoa!"

Smiling, she steadied him. "Let me help." She held his small shoulders so that he could hold the pose. "Why can't you see Micah anymore?"

"He got his forever family."

A thick lump settled in her throat. "His forever family?"

"Yes, ma'am. That means he gets to go live with them forever." He dropped his leg to the ground and squinted up at her. "I almost had a forever family, but then I didn't."

Lindy couldn't answer that, and in spite of the fact that she was glad he hadn't been adopted yet, she was still angry at the people who decided they didn't want her child.

"But Mr. Ethan wants to be my forever daddy," he added with a sweet little grin that pierced her soul.

She swallowed. "He does? How do you know?"

"One of the big kids told me."

Lindy looked across the pebbled pathway that ran through the zoo and spotted Ethan, talking to Candace but looking directly at them. "Do you *want* him to be your forever daddy, Jerry?" she asked, knowing that a court would probably be asking him the same thing in the near future.

"Sure!" His smile inched higher, and her heart squeezed tighter. She'd known what the answer would be, but that didn't make hearing it any easier.

How could she compete with that?

She glanced around to make sure no one was close enough to hear, then she squatted to face the boy she loved more than life itself. "What about a forever mommy, Jerry? Would you want a forever mommy?"

He squinted at her, those adorable freckles sprinkled across his cheeks and drawing even more attention to the same blue eyes she saw each day when she looked in the mirror. "Like who?" he asked with the beautiful innocence of a child.

"Like maybe someone like me." She held her breath and prayed for an answer that wouldn't break her heart.

Those freckles danced with his smile. "Sure!"

It took everything she had to keep from crying in front of her son, but she held it together. "I would like that, too," she said softly.

"Hey, I saw you two take a tumble. Are you okay?" Ethan asked as he and Candace walked toward them.

"Yes, sir," Jerry answered. "We're good, aren't we Miss Lindy?"

"Very good," she said, doing her best to control the happiness flooding through her at Jerry's statement. He wanted a forever mommy, someone like her. Now if he would just tell the judge that, maybe...

"Awesome. I sure didn't want my little man to get hurt," Ethan said, and then looked to Lindy. "Or Miss Lindy."

"Thanks," she said, and then realized that, as far as the court was concerned, Jerry wanting her to be his forever mommy would probably be canceled out by the fact that he also wanted Ethan to be his forever daddy.

"Jerry, I have to leave to go back to work, but I'm so glad I got to see you and spend time with you today," Candace said. "Are you having a good time at the zoo with Mr. Ethan?"

"Yes, ma'am," he said. "And Miss Lindy, too."

Candace smiled. "I see that." She looked to Lindy. "We should talk sometime. After you feel like you're settled in in Claremont, I want you to give me a call." She withdrew a business card from her bag and handed it to Lindy. "I think you were wrong when you said you didn't have anything to offer a child. I'm seeing quite the opposite."

"I can vouch for that, too," Ethan said, giving her a smile that sent butterflies dancing in her stomach. How could she be so attracted to a man who could take her son away?

"You'd be a great mom," he mouthed, and her skin warmed from the encouragement. But she wondered if they would still be saying this if they knew the truth about who she was.

"Thanks," she said, scanning Candace's card before sliding it into her purse.

Dylan jogged toward them. "Hey, Jerr-Bear, I already took the other kids to see the lions' den, but I can take you now, if you want to go. What do you say?"

"Can I?" Jerry asked Ethan.

Not Lindy. Ethan.

Ethan ran a hand across his sandy hair. "Of course. Just bring him back here when y'all are done, Dylan, okay?"

"Yes, sir." Dylan held a hand out to Jerry. "Ready, Jerr-Bear?"

"Ready," Jerry said, taking Dylan's hand and letting him lead him toward the exhibit.

Candace waited until they walked away before speaking. "I saw an exhibit on the other side of the park that would probably be a good place for you to take Jerry."

"What is it?" Ethan asked.

"It's called the Remarkable Parents exhibit," Candace said.

"Oh, I saw that on here." Lindy withdrew the park map from her dress pocket and unfolded it. "It isn't far from here."

Ethan peeked over her shoulder to see the location on the map, and Lindy tried to ignore that appealing spicy scent of his aftershave. Or was it, like she'd suspected before, simply the masculine scent of Ethan? Either way, she attempted not to notice.

It was not an easy feat.

Candace nodded. "Yes, that's it. From what I read about the exhibit, it will show Jerry how parents take care of their children. Often, when I have a family who is going to adopt a child, I ask if they're interested in adopting a puppy. If they want a puppy, of course," she added with a laugh.

"A puppy?" Lindy echoed.

Candace nodded. "It's a great way to show the child how the adoption process works and how they will be loved in the new family. Since Jerry isn't living with you yet, and since you're staying at the Claremont Bed and Breakfast instead of your home, adopting a puppy wouldn't make sense at this point. But I'm thinking you can accomplish the same thing by taking him to that exhibit, answering any questions he may have about the family unit, things like that."

Ethan nodded. "I see what you mean. Sounds like a good idea. We'll head over after Dylan brings him back."

"And let me know how it goes. I'll add any insightful responses on Jerry's part to my report."

"I will," Ethan said, and Lindy suddenly had the impulse to ask the woman to add Jerry's earlier insightful response, that he would like a forever mommy…and that he'd like it to be her. But she kept that to herself for now.

Candace said goodbye and left, and Dylan brought Jerry back from the lion exhibit.

"Show them how the biggest lion went," Dylan said as they neared.

Jerry took a deep breath then did his best impersonation of a lion's roar, his growl hardly fierce but absolutely adorable.

Ethan laughed, and so did Lindy. "Good job," she said.

"It sure is," Ethan said. "So how many lions were there?"

"Four, but two of them were taking a nap, so we didn't get to really see them that good. But the other ones were a mommy and a daddy, and the daddy was the one with a bunch of hair."

"And that bunch of hair is called…" Dylan prompted.

"His mane," Jerry said proudly. "And the mommy one was a lot smaller, and they don't have any babies yet, but the zoo man said that they are going to have some one day. So I guess they aren't a mommy and daddy yet, but just a boy and girl lion."

"Gotcha," Ethan said. "Hey, Miss Candace told us about another place at the zoo that she thought we'd like to see. Want to go see it?"

"Yes, sir!" Jerry said excitedly.

"I'm going to go see some of my friends at the reptile discovery center," Dylan said. "I'll catch you later, Jerr-Bear, okay?" He held out his palm.

"Okay!" Jerry said, slapping it in an exaggerated high five.

Lindy could hardly believe this was the same little boy who had seemed so sad such a short time ago, when she'd first seen him at that fountain on the square. She glanced to Ethan, grinning at the little guy he wanted for a son, and her heart pinched inside. Ethan had been great for Jerry, and she really didn't want to hurt him.

But…he was *her* son.

Ten minutes later, they arrived at the entrance of the Remarkable Parents exhibit, which was unique from the rest of the zoo. This one was an air-conditioned theater, with the buttery, salty smell of popcorn filling the air and teasing them as they entered.

"Can we get some popcorn, Mr. Ethan?" Jerry took a deep breath to enjoy the scent that had practically everyone lining up for an afternoon snack.

"I've never been able to turn down popcorn at a movie," Ethan answered. "Didn't even realize we were going to a movie, but this will be a nice break from the heat, won't it?"

"Definitely," Lindy said, as they moved toward the concession line.

"Do you like butter on yours, or want it plain?" Ethan asked her.

"How did you know I wanted popcorn?"

"If you could smell that and not want popcorn, I'd think something was wrong with you," he said with a grin.

"Good point. But I can buy my own." She unfastened the top of her purse, but Ethan placed his hand on hers.

"Not today. It's my treat." He perused the items on the menu board hanging overhead and was ready when the girl behind the counter asked for his order. "We'd like the family special—two large drinks, one small drink and three popcorns."

"Butter on the popcorn?" the girl asked.

"Lindy, do you like butter on yours?"

Her mind was still swimming from the fact that he'd purchased a family special. "Um, no," she said. "No, thank you."

"I want butter," Jerry said, rising on his tippy-toes to get the girl's attention.

"Is that okay with Daddy?" she asked.

Lindy turned to see Ethan inhale thickly and glance down at Jerry, who hadn't said anything to correct her error.

"Yes, it's fine," he answered.

Lindy's heart plummeted. Had Jerry already started thinking of him as his forever daddy?

Ethan handed her a box of popcorn and a soda, then handed Jerry a "kid pack" that included a small drink, popcorn and a packet of fruit snacks.

"This is awesome!" Jerry said. "Thank you, Mr. Ethan."

Lindy was glad he hadn't called him Daddy… yet.

"Okay then, let's go find out what this movie thing is all about," Ethan said, leading the way and holding open the door to the theater for Lindy and Jerry, their arms filled with popcorn and drinks, to pass through.

"Can you both sit by me?" Jerry asked, picking a row of seats near the top.

"Of course," Ethan said, and he moved past Jerry to sit on his left side, while Lindy took her place on his right.

"Miss Lindy, can you help me with my drink?"

"Sure," she said. She lowered the armrest and placed his drink in the slot. "How's that?"

"Great," Jerry said, wiggling into the seat and then digging into his box of popcorn. He wasted no time putting more than she'd have thought possible in his mouth.

There weren't a lot of people in the theater for this showing. In fact, they were the only ones seated on their aisle. So when she glanced across the row, at Jerry sitting beside her eating popcorn and at Ethan, also eating popcorn, but grinning back at her, she saw them as they probably appeared to anyone who looked at them now.

A sweet little family.

She shouldn't be thinking about that right now. Because as soon as Ethan found out who she was, and as soon as they started the official battle for Jerry, he wouldn't even speak to her, much less want to sit with her and Jerry in a movie.

She forced herself to look away from the two of them, ate a handful of popcorn and sipped her drink. Anything to gather her bearings and stop thinking about things that could never be.

"I like going to the movies," Jerry said, and Lindy was thankful for his distraction.

"You do?" she asked. "Have you been to the movies a lot?"

"No, I only went one time," he said, chomping on his popcorn. "With Daddy Mark and Mama Carol."

"Who are Daddy Mark and Mama Carol?" Ethan asked casually, though Lindy could hear the curiosity in his tone. He wanted to know as badly as she did.

"My old daddy and mama. Not the last one, though." He continued to chew, swallowed and then sipped at his drink. "The last one was Daddy Bill and Mama Janie."

Lindy hated that *Daddy* and *Mama* had become temporary terms in her little boy's world, but at least he knew there was a difference in his "old" mommies and daddies and looked forward to the forever mommy—or forever daddy—he'd mentioned before.

Ethan glanced over Jerry's head and caught her attention, his solemn smile saying he was thinking the same thing. This child had been uprooted too much. He needed stability. She forced a smile, knowing that Ethan would probably take it to mean she agreed that *he* could give Jerry what he needed.

The problem was, she *knew* he could.

And any court would agree.

The lights dimmed, and they all looked toward the curved, full-wall screen that spanned the front of the theater, where a collage of animal photographs tumbled across the display. Each photo depicted the same scene: adult animals caring for their offspring.

Jerry ate another handful of popcorn, loudly slurped his drink through the straw and then pointed to the screen. "Look at that, Mr. Ethan. What is it?" He pointed to the first full image to cover the screen.

Ethan answered, "That's an orangutan."

Jerry giggled around another mouthful of popcorn, swallowed and said, "That's a funny name." He looked at Lindy. "Isn't that a funny name, Miss Lindy?"

"Yes, it is," she said, finding odd comfort in being included in a conversation that could've been between Ethan and the boy he planned to adopt. She thanked God for allowing her to have this day off, and for Ethan being willing to let her share in moments like this with Jerry.

Maybe if she regained custody, she would let Ethan spend time with her son. Jerry truly cared about him, and he'd be sad if Ethan wasn't in his life.

The thought was quickly followed with curiosity—would Ethan do the same for her if *he* won in court?

Once he found out the truth about her past, probably not.

The speakers were extremely loud, so that the narrator's voice seemed to bounce off all walls and the ceiling.

"The most prominent remarkable parent in the animal kingdom is the orangutan. The bond between an orangutan mother and her young is one of the strongest in nature."

The orangutan baby climbed on top of his mother, and she appeared to be kissing him. Several "awws" echoed through the theater.

"During the first two years of life, young orangutans rely entirely on their mothers, not only for food but also for transportation. The moms stay with their offspring for six to seven years, and during that time, the babies learn where to find their food, how to eat it and how to build a place to sleep, which is called their sleeping nest."

The orangutan image faded out, and a group of penguins filled the screen.

"Wow, cool!" Jerry said. "I like penguins."

"The emperor penguins are also an excellent

example of remarkable parents. After laying an egg, the mother emperor penguin leaves it with a male. He then protects the fragile egg from the elements while the baby's mother travels many miles to find fish in the ocean. Later on, she returns to feed the tiny chicks and keep them warm."

"Hey, that penguin mommy catches fish, like we did!" Jerry said excitedly.

"Yes," Ethan said, "but not the same way we did. She doesn't have to use a pole, a hook or a minnow."

Jerry giggled, then watched as more and more animal parents filled the screen.

They listened to three additional stories, of polar bears, African elephants and cheetahs, all of whose parents cared for them extensively through their youth. Lindy could see why Candace had recommended this exhibit. The film underscored the need for a parent to take care of its young, as well as the lengths some parents go to care for their children.

She desperately wanted to be that kind of parent to Jerry.

When the movie ended, Ethan asked, "So what do you think of that, Jerry? Wasn't that cool how the mommies and daddies all took care of their babies?"

Jerry took a big sip of his drink, gobbled

another handful of popcorn and then nodded. "Yes, sir."

Light streamed into the theater as the exit doors automatically opened to reveal the sunlight outside. And the heat of the afternoon seemed even warmer after they'd spent a little time in the air-conditioned theater.

"So that was pretty neat, wasn't it?" Ethan said again as they walked into the heat. "All of those parents and their babies?"

Jerry didn't answer, but instead squinted to adjust to the change in light. "Wow, that sunshine hurts," he said.

Ethan leaned toward Lindy and whispered in her left ear. "I still think it was good for him to see that, don't you?"

The nearness of him as he asked the question, coupled with the fact that this seemed like something two parents would discuss, sent a trickle of goose bumps down both arms. "Yes, I think it was good," she managed to say.

Ethan had slid his sunglasses on as they exited, and Lindy's hat shielded her face, but Jerry held his small hand at his brow to ward off the light. "I'm crying but I'm not sad," he said, confused.

Lindy smiled, thinking he had to be the cutest little boy ever. "Your eyes are just watering a little while they get used to the sunshine. They should be better in a minute."

"I think I saw some sunglasses for kids in the gift shop over there," Ethan said. "Would you like to go pick some out?"

"Yes, sir!" Jerry said, grinning as they started toward the store.

Within minutes, Ethan had purchased a cute pair of sunglasses for Jerry, as well as a stylish pair of women's sunglasses for Lindy, totally ignoring her objections and the fact that she said they were unnecessary since she had the floppy hat.

"There will be days when you don't have your hat around, and you'll be able to use them then," he said as he neared her. "Here, let's make sure they fit okay." Then he gently ran a finger along her left cheek to tuck a long lock of hair behind her ear, before doing the same for the right.

Lindy's goose bumps weren't controllable at the moment, and she prayed he didn't notice the effect he had on her.

"Now let's see how these look." He slid the glasses on, taking care to guide the arms over her ears and situate them comfortably on the bridge of her nose. He nodded when he got them in place. "Perfect," he whispered.

Lindy thought the same thing. This man

seemed so very perfect. And the more time she spent with Ethan Green, the more she believed everything about him. He truly appeared to be the real deal.

"Hey, Jerry, you coming? It's time to get on the bus, and Miss Savvy has Popsicles for us to eat when we get inside, but everyone has to be on the bus before we get them," a dark-skinned boy called to them as he ran past the store.

"I'm coming!" Jerry yelled, then he looked to Ethan and Lindy. "We have to go to the bus," he said.

"That's right," Ethan agreed, checking his watch. "I didn't even realize the time. Come on, Jerry, we'll walk you there."

They all headed there together, Jerry showing everyone along the way his new sunglasses, Ethan and Lindy on either side of him as he practically skipped toward the Willow's Haven bus.

Savvy stood at the bus entrance with a clipboard, checking off the children as they boarded. "Did you have a good day, Jerry?" she asked.

"I had a great day," he said, and then pointed to his red, white and blue sunglasses. "Mr. Ethan got me these."

"Well, wasn't that nice?" she said, smiling.

"Yes, ma'am," he said, and stopped walking just shy of the bus to turn toward Ethan and Lindy. He opened both arms toward Ethan, and Ethan squatted to accept the hug. "Thank you, Mr. Ethan."

Lindy watched the emotion play across Ethan's face as he hugged her son. There was no doubt in her mind he loved Jerry, too.

Then, just as she thought she would have to watch him turn and get on the bus without hugging her, he moved to her, arms out. She swallowed, fought the tears that beckoned for release and lowered to accept a long-awaited hug from her son.

"Thank you, Miss Lindy."

She couldn't stop herself. She kissed his soft cheek and held him for a moment longer than she probably should. "Thank you, Jerry."

"Come on, Jerry," one of the kids called from an open window. "You're the last one, and we're ready for our Popsicles!"

Jerry backed out of her embrace. "I'm coming," he said, grinning, and then darted toward Savvy, who checked off his name. After he had boarded, she turned to Ethan. "I hear it won't be much longer, right?"

"That's what Candace said," he answered.

"That's great, because I can tell he's ready."

She climbed onto the bus and told the kids they could have banana, strawberry or grape Popsicles.

"I think he'll want grape," Ethan said.

"I say strawberry," Lindy countered, and then they watched as Jerry found his way to a window and held up the treat, bright red, for them to see.

Ethan gave him a thumbs-up, and Lindy clapped. "I win."

"Yes, you do," he said, grinning. "How about I get you an ice cream to celebrate? I saw an ice cream stand in the middle of the zoo."

"I saw that too," she said, "but you bought the popcorn and sodas. It's my turn to treat."

He tilted his head, pointed a finger toward her and said, "Yeah, well, that would've been true if you hadn't just won. But you did, so I have no choice but to treat."

"You don't fight fair," she said, but she couldn't keep from smiling.

"Sure, I do," he countered. "Now come on, let's get some ice cream. We need something to cool us off in this heat."

He was right. Today had been the hottest day since she'd come to Claremont, easily in the midnineties, and ice cream would definitely help cool them off. "I wonder if they'll have white chocolate turtle."

He laughed. "White chocolate turtle? I've never heard of it."

"I've heard of it, but I've never tried it. Mrs. Bowers was talking about getting an ice cream freezer at the fishing hole, and asked me to help her pick flavors. That was one of the options, but I had no idea what it tastes like. We got it, but I'm still wondering if it'll be something customers will like." She walked beside him through the park, feeling completely at ease.

"Well, then, you should probably try it," he said, laughing. "As a good employee, it's your obligation."

The ice cream stand had mesh and glass windows under a red-and-white-striped awning. Photos of sundaes, waffle cones, sugar cones and cake cones garnished with mounds of colorful ice cream were placed above each window to tempt customers.

"Do you happen to have a flavor called white chocolate turtle?" Ethan asked the woman behind the mesh window.

"We sure do," she said. "It's one of our two new flavors we added this week—that and banana pudding."

"Banana pudding ice cream?" he asked.

"Yes, sir. Would you like to try a sample?"

"I sure would," he said. "And can Lindy try

a sample of that white chocolate turtle?" He tilted his head toward her.

"Of course!" She moved toward the freezers that lined the center of the stand, grabbed a couple of red plastic spoons and then filled each with a small sample of the two flavors.

Lindy waited while he took the two spoons, handed her one and then tried his own and smiled.

"Banana pudding is a winner in my book. It even has the Nilla wafers in it. Can't beat that. I'll take a double scoop in a brown-sugar cone, please." He nodded toward her spoon, and she slipped it into her mouth to taste.

Bliss.

"Oh. Wow." She wasn't certain she'd ever tried an ice cream that tasted so amazing. However, she hadn't had *any* ice cream during her time at Tutwiler, or since her release.

No wonder this tasted so great.

"That good, huh?" he asked. "I take it you want that kind then?"

"Definitely," she said.

"How many scoops and what kind of cone?" the girl behind the window asked.

"A cake cone please," she said. "And a single scoop."

"A single?" Ethan asked. "That's just enough to make you want more. You need a double."

"After popcorn and soda?" she asked.

"Of course," he said. "This is dessert."

The teen behind the mesh giggled, and Lindy laughed. "Oh, okay then. A double scoop."

"You got it," the girl said, and turned to fix their cones.

"You're going to be one of those parents, aren't you?" Lindy asked. "Spoiling your kid rotten?"

His face suddenly grew serious, and he answered, "You know, Jerry could stand a little spoiling for a while, after all he's been through, so yeah, I probably will. But I won't overdo it. I've been thinking about that a lot lately, getting the right balance, because the judge will probably ask my thoughts on parenting. For now, though, I will tend to say yes a little more than no." He raised a shoulder. "'Cause I think he needs some extra love, you know?"

Lindy hadn't actually been referring to Jerry, but to parenting in general. But his explanation, as well as why he wanted to give Jerry a little more, made perfect sense. And touched her heart.

He really would be a good daddy to her son, and she supposed if the court didn't see fit to give Jerry back to her, then she'd want him to be with someone like Ethan.

No, not someone *like* Ethan. She would indeed want him to be with Ethan if he couldn't be with her.

As much as that would hurt.

"Here you go," the girl said, sliding the mesh aside and handing the cones to Ethan and Lindy. "One double scoop of banana pudding on a brown-sugar cone, and a double scoop of white chocolate turtle in a cake cone."

"That's a double?" Lindy asked. The lumps of ice cream towered above the small cone. She'd have counted it as a triple, at least.

"We try to give you your money's worth."

"Awesome," Ethan said, fishing out his wallet.

"Hang on, and I'll get your change," she said.

"Nah, keep that for your tip. You really outdid yourself on these scoops."

She smiled. "Thanks!"

Ethan pointed to a picnic area under some trees nearby. "How about eating over there?"

"Looks great," Lindy said, already working on her ice cream. In this heat, it would melt quickly.

He grabbed a small stack of napkins from a dispenser and led the way to one of the concrete circular tables that had a bright red umbrella, providing extra shade beneath the trees.

They started on their ice cream cones without talking, and Lindy considered that they might enjoy them in silence, without speaking of the adoption, or their day with Jerry. But she couldn't stand it. She wanted to know what Candace had said and what Ethan knew about her request to move up the court date.

So she said, "I'd never heard of people adopting a puppy to show kids what it means to be adopted, but that seems like a good idea."

"Yeah," he said, making a lot more headway in his ice cream than Lindy. "I'd have adopted one for sure if we were at home in Birmingham. I've actually always wanted a dog, but never really felt a reason to get one. Didn't know if I'd be neglecting it too much when I was at school."

"We always had a dog growing up, me and my grandmother, and I can't imagine being a kid and not having one." She licked at her ice cream as fast as she could, but it still dribbled down the sides of her cone.

"Well, I've already decided that once we get back to Birmingham, I'll take Jerry to the pound and let him pick a puppy for us to keep. That way I can still talk to him about adopting a puppy the same way I'm adopting him."

Lindy grabbed a few of the napkins, swiped at the ice cream streaming down her cone and then continued eating—while picturing Ethan and Jerry picking out a puppy together.

Another first that could potentially be his instead of hers.

If the court ruled in his favor.

"Did Candace say anything about the adoption?" she asked, trying to keep her tone relaxed, as though she weren't at all concerned about the answer. Which couldn't be further from the truth.

"Yes, she did," he said, and Lindy was surprised to see that he'd eaten all of the ice cream from the top and was now working on the cone. "Turns out we could be going to court sooner than we thought."

"That's…good news, right?"

"It can be," Ethan said. "As long as we get a judge who will look at what's best for Jerry."

"Because Candace thinks a judge will decide you're best for him."

He tossed the end of the cone in his mouth. "I can't imagine them not seeing that, especially since his mother didn't protect him back then."

"Maybe she tried." Lindy hoped her words wouldn't give away her identity, but she had to open the door to the possibility that Jerry's mother did care, that she did love him and had tried her best to protect him.

Because that was the truth.

"She didn't," he said flatly.

"How do you know?" She took another swipe at her ice cream, but it no longer tasted good.

"Because I've been there," he said again, with hardly any emotion. "I've seen a mother stand by and allow someone to hurt her child. No woman like that deserves her son. Surely the court will agree."

Unless it's a judge who believes in family reunification, or believes me when I say I did try, Lindy thought. But she only said, "Maybe so."

"Those animals in the movie showed how a mother should protect her young. Jerry's mother didn't do that, and he deserves to know what that's like, to have someone love you that much, care about you that much. I want to do that for him."

"I do, too," she said honestly, and then, when his brow lifted, she said, "I want to do that for a child, I mean."

"You're going to be a great mother, Lindy. And Candace was serious about you contacting her. She'll help you adopt. I feel certain of it." He smiled and pointed to her dripping cone. "You're losing the majority of your ice cream."

Regardless of how delicious the white chocolate turtle was, she had no desire for it anymore. "I'm done."

"Care if I try it?" he asked.

She swallowed and extended the cone, half

a scoop still towering above the rim. "You can have it."

Then she watched him take the cone and begin eating the remainder of the ice cream, as though it were completely natural for them to be sitting here, sharing not only conversation but also an ice cream cone.

It didn't matter that the temperature had climbed even higher. A waterfall of goose bumps spilled down her arms *and* her legs. What was it about this man?

"Candace said it shouldn't be longer than two weeks," he said, "before we meet with the judge. Two weeks…and I may have a son." The top of the ice cream gone, he took a bite of the cone. "We'll have to celebrate when that happens. How about it—another ice cream date when the adoption goes through?" His smile touched her heart, but his words haunted her soul.

Would he be celebrating? Or would she?

"What do you say, is it a date?" he asked.

A date. With Ethan. To celebrate Jerry's adoption.

"Come on. It'll definitely be a cause for celebration. Ice cream again, and we'll bring Jerry along, of course. Say yes, Lindy. I like spending time with you, and I want you to be a part of this, if everything goes through the way Candace believes it will. Let's celebrate Jerry's adoption together. Say yes."

She prayed she would be the one celebrating. "Okay. Yes."

Chapter Ten

Ten days after the trip to the zoo, Ethan got the call he'd been waiting for. He hung up the phone with Candace early Monday morning and immediately said a prayer of thanks. Two weeks. He only had to wait two more weeks until the court hearing, thanks to Melinda Sue Flinn's request to expedite the case.

"Thank you, Melinda Sue."

"Now, I know good and well that you know my name, and it certainly isn't Melinda Sue," Annette Tingle said, placing a plate filled with bananas Foster French toast that smelled absolutely incredible in front of him.

He laughed. "Sorry, I was talking to myself."

"Now, you're way too young to start that already," she said, putting a tiny crystal syrup dispenser near his plate. "You need to be my age before you start that nonsense. I do it all the time. Thankfully, L.E. doesn't tease me overly much. Of course, that'd be hard to do since I catch him talking to himself every day, as well." She chuckled as she poured fresh-squeezed orange juice into his glass and then hot coffee into his mug.

"So who is this Melinda Sue that you're thanking?" she asked. "Or if that's none of my beeswax, you just say so."

"I don't mind telling you," he said. "Melinda Sue is Jerry's birth mother, and she's trying to get custody of him again. She asked for the court hearing to be moved up, and the state granted her request." He poured the warm syrup over the French toast and considered that if he stuck around the B and B much longer, he'd have to develop a new workout regimen to combat the calories.

"Hmm," Mrs. Tingle said. "Do you think she did that because she's missing her little boy, or is there another reason?"

"The social worker thinks she did it to try to keep me from having time to bond with Jerry, and I agree."

Since he was currently the sole guest at the B and B, she sat at the table across from him. "I'd say she missed the mark on that one, then. You two are as tight as two peas in a pod, as far as I can tell. And I've gotta tell you, it was adorable to see him sitting with you and Lindy on Sunday morning at church."

That had been Ethan's doing. He'd been waiting for Jerry when the Willow's Haven bus arrived at the Claremont Community Church, and then, when Lindy had shown up shortly after, he'd asked Jerry if he wanted to ask her to sit with them.

They'd been spending quite a bit of time together over the past few weeks, and it felt right, her being with him when he and Jerry were together. More…complete. And Ethan was tired of denying that fact. He also wasn't going to pretend that he only liked having her around for Jerry's sake.

It was her undeniable appeal…to Ethan.

"It was nice to sit with them," he said.

"Mmm-hmm." She watched him as he took another bite of French toast.

Ethan knew she had something on her mind, something that involved him and Lindy. And probably Jerry. But he decided to bypass her scrutiny. "This is amazing, but I really don't want you to go to all this trouble when I'm the only one here. Like I've told you before, I usually eat a bowl of cereal or a bagel with peanut butter when I'm home."

"And like I've told you, you are paying for a bed-and-breakfast. Cereal or a bagel doesn't count as a real breakfast in my book. What would you do if someone who knew you were staying at the B and B asked what you ate this morning, and I had served cold cereal?" Her tone was incredulous.

"I'd tell them I had cereal?" he answered, but when she huffed out a breath, added, "and that I liked it."

"No, indeed." She shook her head with gusto. "Well, you *won't* be telling anyone that, because I'll *never* serve cold cereal in my kitchen."

He gave her a mock salute. "Yes, ma'am." Then he took a sip of her rich, dark coffee. Everything she served was outstanding.

"And when you do go back home, if you have that little boy with you—and I think you will— you should make certain he has a real breakfast each morning. That's the most important meal of the day, and it'll help him do better in school."

"You sound sure about that," he said, moving back to the food on his plate and taking another delicious bite.

"I read it online."

He smirked, swallowed. "Then it must be true."

"I believe it." She leaned forward and put her fingertips together on the table in front of her. "And I believe something else, too."

He could almost see the wheels churning. She had something on her mind and was trying to bring the conversation around to where she wanted it. "What's that?"

"I believe you shouldn't be raising that little boy alone. Me and Jolaine have been talking about it, and we're both under the impression that you need a wife."

Unfortunately, Ethan had just taken another mouthful of syrupy toast, and he swallowed so quickly that he choked. He coughed, eyes watering, while she merely shook her head and smiled.

"So I need a wife," he said, playing along.

"Yes, you do. Definitely."

"Because you and Mrs. Bowers think I do," he continued, enjoying the thought of the two women discussing and planning his future. He'd never really had anyone besides Daddy Jim and Mama Reba who cared that much about his direction in life. And he'd never had anyone concerned about his relationship status. So this felt very…nice.

"We do," she said, nodding her head, "and I'll just tell you, we're usually pretty good judges about these things."

"Oh, Mrs. Bowers mentioned something to that effect the other day," he said, using his fork to run a piece of toast around the syrup and then sticking a slice of banana on the end before putting the delicious bite into his mouth.

A great breakfast and fun company. He could get used to this.

"We also know *who* you should marry, in case she hasn't told you yet."

This time, his laugh bubbled free. "Do tell."

Blue eyes twinkled as though she were enjoying this comical banter even more than Ethan. "Why, it's Miss Lindy, of course. She's perfect for you. It's obvious that you two care about each other. I mean, you should have seen how good y'all looked in that pew at church."

He couldn't control his laughter. "Which is undeniably something to look for in a mate— how they look sitting next to you on a church pew."

"It certainly doesn't hurt," she deadpanned.

Mercy, he was enjoying this.

"And she loves that little boy. You can see it on her face when she looks at him. I'd say, in fact, that she probably loves him as much as you do. Which would make her great wife material, because y'all would be raising him together."

He grinned, polished off the last of his French toast and then went for a couple of stray banana slices hovering in syrup.

"I think you should consider it, especially

before you leave town and lose the chance to see her so often. She's a beautiful young lady. I'm sure you've noticed that. And she's sweet and hard-working, great with kids… Girls like that don't stay single long."

He pushed the plate forward and took a long sip of the fresh-squeezed orange juice, which was, as it had been every other day, delicious. "I'll take that into consideration."

She plopped both elbows on the table, pressed her chin into her palms and gave him what could only be called her best glare. "Okay. I'm just going to say what's on my mind."

Ethan grinned. He was pretty sure she'd been doing that all morning. "Okay, shoot."

"Are you going to ask her out or not?"

Easy question. Easy answer. "I already did."

She clapped her hands together. "Now, that's what I'm talking about. I'm going to call Jolaine and tell her." And then she was out of the room in a flash, and within seconds, he heard her chatting away with her friend about another well-made match on their part.

He was glad the women were happy, but if he were being honest, he hadn't planned on asking Lindy out at all. He'd *planned* to keep his distance. But when they'd been sharing that ice cream and talking about Jerry's adoption, it seemed completely natural to want her to celebrate with them. She'd been a big part of their journey since day one, so she should be there if and when his adoption went through.

And truthfully, he couldn't wait. He'd found himself thinking about Lindy Burnett nonstop since he'd first seen her at the fountain on the square, and even more after spending so much time with her and Jerry. She stirred feelings within him that he thought might have been gone for good, and he wasn't fighting the pull any longer. In fact, when Mrs. Tingle had mentioned that whole "need a wife" thing, he hadn't balked inside the way he'd have done merely a couple of months ago.

On the contrary, his mind had headed to one place. His home. With Jerry. And, if she felt the same way…with a beautiful strawberry blonde who was slowly but surely taking complete control of his heart.

Lindy walked down the stairs from her room at six thirty Monday morning to find Mrs. Bowers hanging up the phone and smiling from ear to ear. "Good morning, dear. How did you sleep?"

She'd dreamed all night about every life-changing moment she'd experienced over the past three years. The moment the police had arrived at the women's shelter and she'd learned

Gil had been murdered. The moment she'd learned she was the prime suspect, and her baby boy was pulled from her arms. The moment she'd heard the jury foreman pronounce her guilty. The moment she'd learned that her case had been overturned. The moment she'd finally seen her little boy again. And the moment Ethan had looked at her and asked her to help him celebrate Jerry's adoption…and she'd said yes.

He'd brought up their "future date" several times since that day, which underscored the importance of the court date to Ethan. And to Lindy. Because truthfully, since he'd shown up at the fishing hole every day it was open, regardless of whether it was his day to fish with the kids, she and Ethan hadn't spent too many days that couldn't potentially be considered dates.

And to her complete surprise, she was okay with that. Very okay, in fact. Which made the truth of what would happen in a courtroom in two weeks even more distressing.

Mrs. Bowers chuckled. "Does the fact that you aren't answering mean you slept well?"

"To be honest, I didn't," she admitted. And she suspected she wouldn't…for at least fourteen days.

The lady's smile never wavered. "Aw, that's

too bad," she said, shuffling across the small kitchen at the back of the store to smother Lindy with a hug. She rubbed Lindy's back, the way a mother or grandmother would do, and it touched Lindy more than words could express. "Things are going to get better soon, dear. I can just feel it."

Lindy prayed she was right. They would either get much better, or much worse.

Two weeks until she'd hopefully have Jerry in her life again. Or lose him for good. And until she'd promised she'd have a celebratory ice cream "date" with Ethan. A date that should include her son. And a date that would never happen in this lifetime.

Either way the judge ruled, they wouldn't be celebrating together. And that hit her heart hard. She'd so enjoyed spending time with the two of them the past few weeks, at the fishing hole and the town square and the zoo, and especially at church. Yesterday they'd sat there together as though they were a real family.

It'd felt so normal. And her life since meeting Gil had never been anything remotely resembling normal.

Her feelings toward Ethan Green were growing stronger by the day, maybe even by the minute. He made her happy. And, bizarrely, made her believe in the possibility of love again.

She cringed. He would hate her when this was over.

As if she knew where Lindy's thoughts had headed, Mrs. Bowers leaned back from the hug, looked her in the eye and said, "That young man cares about you, child. I could see it all over him yesterday at church, and I'm pretty sure you can tell, too."

Lindy nodded, too spent to disagree. Plus, she thought the lady was right.

"You care about him, too, don't you?" she continued.

Lindy nodded again, trying not to cry. This would end in such an awful way. She kept hearing Ethan's words, first from that day at the zoo and repeated several times since.

You're going to be a great mother, Lindy.

Would he still be saying that when he learned the truth?

"Hey now," Mrs. Bowers said, "I have no idea what causes you to doubt that you can be happy, but you can. And I have a strong suspicion Ethan Green is a big part of making that happen." She touched a finger to Lindy's cheek. "Why are you so worried?"

"My past," Lindy whispered. "You couldn't understand…"

The woman shook her head and tsked. "That's fear talking, honey, and you need to stop listening to it. Fear says the past is your prison. God says the past is your classroom." She gave Lindy a soft smile. "Promise me you'll think about that, okay?"

Lindy had a bizarre urge to laugh at the lady's use of the word *prison*. If she only knew. "Thank you for that. And thank you for everything. I don't know what I'd be doing now without you and Mr. Bowers's help."

"We just let the good Lord lead our steps, dear, and He's got His hand on you. I can see that, too."

Lindy prayed she was right.

"And today should be a great day at the fishing hole for you and for all of the mentors and mentees," Mrs. Bowers continued. "We're bringing some of those new pedal boats out this morning. James has already got the truck loaded, and we should be heading that way shortly to get them ready for the kids."

Lindy thought about that first day she'd seen Jerry, and the way he'd looked at that pedal boat in the store's display window. He wanted to try it, but he'd been scared. And she thought she knew why.

"I was thinking that I would ride out with James this morning and then stay and work at the fishing hole today, if that's okay with you."

Lindy had really wanted to be there when

Jerry tried the pedal boat. "You want me to stay here and work the store today?" she asked, doing her best to hide her disappointment.

"Oh no, James will get back in plenty of time before it opens. I was thinking that I could run the store at the fishing hole today, and you could enjoy the day with the Willow's Haven group. Make sure they're all having a good time."

Lindy was beginning to understand this lady well enough to know what she was really trying to do. "You're giving me another day to spend with Ethan and Jerry."

She waved a hand. "You could put it that way if you want to, but you'll still be working for us, any way you look at it. You're helping us make sure all of our customers are happy. That's part of your job, too, you know."

Lindy swallowed thickly. "I don't know what to say."

"'Thank you' usually works," she answered with a light giggle and a pat to Lindy's cheek.

"Thank you, Mrs. Bowers."

"Why, you're welcome," she said, releasing Lindy from the embrace and giving her a comforting smile. "Now why don't you let me fix you a little breakfast before you head to work?"

"I'm anxious to get to the fishing hole and

get things ready," Lindy said. "But I'll take an apple along for the drive."

"Pfft, that's not enough to start your day," she said, frowning. "I've got some fresh eggs from the Cutters' farm. Why don't you let me fix you a couple? And I have some of my home-made sourdough bread and blackberry jelly to go along with it."

Lindy smiled. "That sounds delicious, but I do want to get to the fishing hole early, espe-cially if the kids will be trying out the pedal boats today. I'll need to have plenty of life jack-ets ready, right?"

"Right," she said, then winked at Lindy. "You are a great employee, you know that?"

"Am I?"

"Yes, dear, you are. And if you won't let me fix you a real breakfast, here's an apple." She picked a big red apple from the fruit bowl on the counter and handed it to Lindy. "I'll be out there soon to take over in the store so you can enjoy some time on the water with your two guys."

Her two guys. She really liked the sound of that—even if it was only temporary.

Chapter Eleven

Ethan had never arrived at the fishing hole before Lindy, but today, he stood waiting on the front porch when she pulled up. He watched as she parked, turned off the ignition…and looked directly at him. This time, she didn't ignore him or give him a half wave. Quite the opposite—she held her hand up and gave him that full smile that caused his heart to lurch in his chest.

Yep, he had it bad.

He placed the bag of breakfast on one of the small tables near the front door, jumped past the porch steps and headed toward the car. "Quilts in the backseat?" he asked, opening the back door on the passenger's side to scoop up the freshly laundered stack that she carried in each morning.

She climbed out of the car and opened the

opposite back door to reach in and grab the rest of the quilts.

They ended up leaning into the car at the same time, locking eyes over the stack of quilts. He grinned, surprised by how happy he could feel simply seeing her. "Hey," he said.

If possible, her smile got a little brighter. "Hey."

A loud rumble sounded in the distance, and they both scooped up some quilts as James Bowers approached in his pickup truck, with a long flatbed trailer attached and loaded down with colorful pedal boats. Jolaine sat in the passenger seat waving excitedly and pointing toward the back of the truck, as if they couldn't see the cargo.

Lindy waved at the pair while Ethan gave them a thumbs-up.

"Jerry is going to be so stoked," he said as they walked toward the porch with the quilts.

She glanced toward the truck as it neared. "I hope so."

"Don't you remember how he said he wanted to try it?"

"I do, but I also remember that he changed his mind." She waited while he opened one of the cedar chests for her to put her quilts in.

Ethan was glad she'd stopped objecting to him helping her. He'd resolved to pursue a relationship of some sort with her over the past few days, and he didn't want to leave Claremont without letting her know that was something he wanted. Very much. Maybe they'd get a chance to talk more today, and he could tell her.

Jolaine and Annette would be proud of themselves, since he had no doubt they'd take total credit for yet another successful match in their books.

He laughed as he placed his stack of colorful quilts beside Lindy's in the chest.

"What is it?" she asked.

"Just thinking about something Mrs. Tingle said this morning." He pointed toward the bag on the table. "I brought another breakfast plate for you today. I'm the only one at the B and B right now, and she said she fixed way too much for her and Mr. Tingle. According to Mrs. Tingle, bananas Foster French toast doesn't taste as good as leftovers, so she *had* to send some." He grinned. "But I'm thinking she just made that up to make sure I brought you breakfast."

Lindy peeked inside the bag. "It looks amazing, but I still need to get everything ready for the kids, and I only have a half hour before they'll be here."

"No worries at all, dear," Mrs. Bowers said, walking toward the porch. "I'm ready to get to work. You enjoy some real breakfast." She gave Lindy her trademark wink.

"But I haven't even set up yet. I haven't got the life jackets ready, made coffee, iced the water bottles."

"I'm pretty sure I can do all of that," Ethan said to Mrs. Bowers. "You can stay with your husband and the pedal boats. I don't mind helping Lindy out here."

"Wonderful," Mrs. Bowers said. "Then I'll go help James get the pedal boats ready for the kids." She also took a peek in the bag from the B and B. "I have *got* to get that banana Foster French toast recipe from Annette." She glanced at Lindy. "Now, that's a real breakfast." Then she left and headed toward the small dock and loading ramp at one end of the pond, where James had already started putting the pedal boats in the water.

Lindy lifted the lid off the box, and the scent of bananas, brown sugar and cinnamon filled the air. "You keep feeding me like this, and I'm going to be huge."

He grinned. "You'd still be beautiful."

As expected, her cheeks turned pink with the compliment.

"Now enjoy your breakfast," he said, "while I go ice down that water and get the coffee brewing. Oh, and where are the life jackets? I'll start getting them ready."

"In the big red bins near the back of the store."

"Good deal. I'm on it." He turned to head inside and get started.

"Ethan?"

He stopped, one hand on the door. "Yeah?"

She swallowed. "Are you really as nice as you seem?"

That made him laugh...until he realized she was dead serious. He cleared his throat. "I do my best," he said, and this time he waited before going in, sensing that she was about to say more.

She waited a beat, then continued, "Mrs. Bowers said something to me this morning. She didn't look at him as she unwrapped the fork from the napkin. "And I was wondering what you'd think about it."

"What did she say?" he asked, assuming it was probably similar to what Mrs. Tingle had said to him, and wondering how he'd respond if she announced that Jolaine and Annette were already planning their wedding.

"She said that fear says your past is your prison, but God says your past is your classroom." She finally looked up, those blue eyes searching his and looking for a response to a statement he hadn't expected. What had happened to her in her past? And how could he convince her that it didn't matter to him now? "What do you think of that?"

Ethan had no doubt that his answer could affect any future relationship with this woman he'd started craving so deeply. And he wanted to give her complete honesty. "I think she's right," he said, "and I don't think anyone should judge you based on your past, Lindy."

"What if…" She put her fork into a banana slice but then hesitated. "What if your past affected someone else's future?"

He could see the torment on her face. Whatever had brought her running to the tiny town of Claremont on her own, without any job, family or home still haunted her. "Lindy, you don't ever have to tell me what happened before. That doesn't matter to me."

"It might," she said, as the Willow's Haven bus came into view in the distance.

"Listen, you eat your breakfast while I go get everything ready inside. We'll talk some more about this later, okay?"

"Okay," she said, finally taking a bite of her food.

Ethan headed inside, got everything ready for the kids…and prayed.

God, please, whatever is hurting her from

her past, let her move beyond it somehow. You know how much I care for her. Help me be what she needs to move beyond her pain.

Lindy could only eat half of the breakfast, in spite of the fact that it was at least as good as, maybe better than, the apple puff pastry Ethan had brought her last week. She wasn't sure whether that was because she was actually full, or because she was simply too nervous to eat.

He'd called her beautiful.

Her skin still tingled from the way that one word from Ethan made her feel, and the thought of telling him about her past weighed heavy on heart. But based on what he'd just said, he didn't care about what happened before she came to Claremont. He didn't even need her to tell him.

Unfortunately, that wasn't an option. She could either tell him—or wait for him to find out when they were in court. And she'd decided it would be better to get the truth out there and give him time to process it before they ended up in a judge's chambers. Maybe that would give him time to forgive her.

Or maybe that would give him time to come up with all the reasons she shouldn't have custody of her son, and convince the judge of the same thing.

God, please help me.

"Hey, Miss Lindy!" Jerry's precious voice carried as he ran toward the porch. "Miss Savvy said we're going to do something extrafun here today. Do you know what it is?"

The Willow's Haven bus had parked on the opposite side of the store from the pond, so the kids hadn't yet seen all of the pedal boats in the water.

"I believe I do," she said.

"What is it?" he asked, as another little boy ran around the store and then darted back.

"Jerry! They got pedal boats!" he yelled.

Jerry's smile wavered. "Pedal boats?"

"Yep," the other boy said. "Come on and pick the one you want!"

"Okay." His tone held no enthusiasm.

Lindy scooped up her bag and tossed it in a trash can nearby. "Jerry, would you rather not try the pedal boats today? Because I don't have to work in the store, and I could sit with you and Mr. Ethan while you fish, if you'd rather do that."

His sandy eyebrows dipped, eyes narrowed and lips grew tight as he considered this. Then he said, "I want to try it, but…will you do it with me?"

She didn't hesitate. "Of course I will." He had a fear, she could see that, but he wanted to face it, and he wanted her help in doing it.

"Hey, Jerry," Ethan said, exiting the store with three life jackets hanging from his right arm. "I got us some life jackets, so we'll be ready to go."

"All of us?" he asked.

"Sure," Ethan said.

"And you're coming, too, Miss Lindy, right?" he asked.

"Of course I am," she said.

"Let's go get our spot at the pond then," Ethan said.

"I want to check inside and make sure Mrs. Bowers doesn't need any help," Lindy said, "and then I'll be right there. You two can go ahead and pick a boat."

"How does that sound, Jerry?" Ethan asked. "Want to go pick which boat you want?"

"I want a red one," Jerry said, taking Ethan's hand and letting him lead him around the house.

"Well, then, let's go see if they have any red ones left." Ethan grinned at Lindy before they rounded the corner, and she thought how perfect they looked, like father and son, heading to the lake.

Would he be Jerry's father soon?

And if he was, where would that leave her?

* * *

Ethan led Jerry to the pier, where mentors and kids donned life jackets and climbed into the pedal boats. Some were already out and about on the water, the colorful boats adding another splash of beauty to the picturesque scene.

While they waited their turn in line, Ethan admired the incredible view. The water seemed closer to a lake than a pond, at least three acres amid vivid green moss-covered banks and soft emerald grass. Sunlight sparkled off the surface, as still as glass, except for where the pedal boats trudged through and a few ripples were created by jumping fish or slow-swimming turtles. The branches of the weeping willow trees cascaded like large mushrooms along the bank's edge, casting lacy shadows across the water. And now that he knew what the fish liked, he suspected all of those shady spots held an abundance of the silver-scaled bream that Jerry loved to catch. Ethan, too, truth be told, now that he knew what he was doing.

Purple irises and lemon-yellow daffodils provided bursts of color around the banks, and thick lily pads with pale pink blooms brought equally mesmerizing hues to the water's surface.

It'd be an incredible setting for a wedding.

He shook his head at where his mind had wandered. All he had to do was see Lindy, or talk to Mrs. Tingle, and he started having thoughts of forever.

Shockingly, those thoughts no longer terrified him.

However, Lindy's question this morning bothered him immensely.

Are you really as nice as you seem?

Who had hurt her so badly that she couldn't trust a simple gesture of kindness? And why did her past continue to haunt her? Her comment about it being a prison or a classroom told him plenty. One, whatever she'd been running from when she came to Claremont was probably even worse than he'd feared. And two, she'd rather not share it, with him or anyone else.

Which was okay. He didn't have to know her past to have her in his future.

But that didn't keep him from wanting to mend those old wounds and see her truly living without fear.

God, help me do that for her.

"So, can we get a red one?" Lindy asked, walking down the bank toward the pier. She wore a pale pink sundress today, the soft, loose fabric nearly reaching her ankles. Always so feminine. And always so beautiful, as he'd told her earlier. It was obvious she wasn't used to hearing that kind of compliment, but she might as well get used to it. Because he intended to tell her often.

He grinned at her and pointed ahead, where Mr. Bowers had the next pedal boat, bright cherry-colored with white seats, waiting. "We got a red one," Ethan said.

"That's what you wanted, right, Jerry?" she asked.

He nodded, but his mouth was drawn tight, and his feet stayed planted firmly on the pier.

"Here you go, Jerry." Mr. Bowers extended a hand. "I'll help you get in."

Jerry shook his head, looked at Ethan then at Lindy. "I'm—I don't know if I want to."

Lindy crouched down, her dress swirling around her as she looked into his future son's eyes and said softly, "Jerry, if you don't want to go, you don't have to. But if you do want to go, and just need a little help, I can hold your hand while you get on the boat."

He looked up at Ethan. "Will you hold my hand, too?"

Ethan reached for his small hand, placed it within his own. "I won't let go," he promised.

Jerry put his other hand in Lindy's and then looked up at Mr. Bowers. "Okay."

"Looks like they've got you covered there, don't they?" the man said with a wink.

"Yes, sir," Jerry answered, but his voice quivered on the last word.

Lindy stood, and she and Ethan guided him to the boat, both of them encouraging him every step of the way.

"Great job," she said, and then, "See, it wobbles a little, but then it settles right down. We're going to have so much fun."

Ethan watched the play of emotions on the little boy's face. There was anxiety, but also courage. In spite of a fear that Ethan couldn't understand, Jerry was determined to accomplish what he wanted to do.

Ethan's admiration for the child swelled. He wasn't going to be afraid to face things in life, and he'd have Ethan there to help him. He looked at the other person guiding him. Lindy's hand was wrapped around Jerry's, and her eyes were filled with tears.

She cared so much.

They made their way into the water, with Ethan and Lindy working the foot pedals, Jerry clutching one hand to the handle while waving to his friends in other boats with the other.

"Are you okay, Jerry?" Lindy asked, for about the sixth time. Ethan was touched by how much she wanted to make sure he was having a good time.

"Yes, ma'am."

The ride went fairly smoothly, until all of the mentors and mentees were in the water. Then the surface grew choppy, and at one point, when two pedal boats going opposite directions neared them, they began to sway in the water.

"Whoa," Jerry said, grabbing Ethan's forearm in a death grip. "Daddy, help."

Ethan's words lodged in his throat, emotion blocking his effort to speak. But his little boy needed him. And he'd called him daddy. "It's okay, Jerry. I'm right here." He heard Lindy sniff, saw her wipe tears away, obviously as touched as Ethan by the tender term of endearment. "We're right here."

The boat eventually calmed, and Jerry's grip on his arm loosened. "We're…okay," he said.

"Yes," Ethan agreed. "We are." Then he wrapped an arm around Jerry's shoulders and squeezed. "I'll take care of you, Jerry, always. You know that, right?"

"Yes, sir."

Ethan squeezed his shoulders once more. "Okay then, ready to head back to the pier?"

"Yes, sir."

Still overwhelmed at hearing his son call him daddy for the first time, Ethan paddled toward the pier. Lindy also paddled, but the two of them didn't speak. He assumed she was probably consumed with the same thoughts, that they'd just heard Jerry call him what he'd be calling him forever…in two short weeks.

Ethan couldn't wait.

By the time they reached the pier, Lindy had wiped countless tears away, always turning her head so that Jerry didn't notice. But Ethan did. And he thought even more of her for her sensitive heart.

Mr. Bowers stood at the pier, directing each of the mentors as he instructed them on how to get their pedal boats out of the water. They waited their turn at the end of the line, but Ethan didn't want Jerry and Lindy to have to remain in the boat in the heat, so he eased closer to the pier. "Why don't y'all go get a couple of those Popsicles from the store while you're waiting for me to put the pedal boat away?"

"Okay!" Jerry said, grinning, and Ethan was glad to see a genuine, nonfearful smile on his little face.

"What flavor do you want?" Lindy asked.

"Grape," Ethan said.

"Grape for Daddy," Jerry said, and no one corrected him. Then he turned to Lindy. "What flavor do you want, Mommy?"

Ethan watched her face as she went through

the same emotions he'd experienced merely a moment ago. Shock. Happiness. *Joy.*

And then he watched her reel it all in and answer.

"Um, I think I want strawberry, Jerry," she said throatily. "Thank you for asking."

Ethan smiled at her and saw that her eyes were swimming with tears once again, but she kept them unshed for the little boy who had touched them both so much.

And he no longer held any doubt. This incredible lady, the one who'd captured his interest that very first day at the fountain and captured his heart in the days and weeks since, was meant to be a part of his life…and Jerry's.

"We'll go get the Popsicles and meet you at the picnic area under the trees," Lindy said, her voice still thick with emotion. "Sound good?"

He nodded. Somehow, he needed Lindy Burnett in his life. He just had to determine how to make that happen.

"Sounds great."

Mommy. Lindy had prayed to hear that term of endearment, from that precious little voice, for three long years. And the emotions she felt now were as poignant as she'd expected. Her heart yearned to hold that special place in her son's life once more, to have him look to her for safety, for comfort, for love.

Love. Love overpowered her right now, flooding through every part of her being, so much that her mouth trembled, her eyes beckoned with tears, her soul rejoiced.

Mommy. Such a beautiful, beautiful word.

She walked beside this little man, her son, and went through the motions of buying the Popsicles, then walking alongside him while they moved toward the picnic tables, Jerry chatting about how awesome the pedal boat had been and Lindy replaying the moment she'd finally heard him call her what she desperately longed to be once more.

By the time they reached the table and started eating their Popsicles, she hadn't been able to hold back the tears.

But Jerry, so wrapped up in the excitement of the day, didn't notice that she'd swiped at each cheek repeatedly while nibbling at the cold treat.

Until he'd finished his Popsicle. "Why are you sad?" he asked, frowning.

"I—I'm not sad," she managed. "I promise."

His mouth quirked to the side, and he scrambled off the concrete bench to dart toward a tree nearby. Then he leaned down and yanked something from the ground.

Lindy watched as he turned, his mouth lifting in a grin, and walked toward her with the most beautiful golden daffodil clutched between his hands.

"This will make you happy," he said.

She blinked, more tears spilling over, but she also found a smile. "You know what? You're right," she said. "It does, Jerry. It makes me so very happy. *You* make me happy, more than you could ever know."

"I love you, Mommy."

As if him calling her Mommy wasn't enough, he'd just given her the most exquisite gift of all. He *loved* her.

And she loved him.

She couldn't wait any longer. She had to tell him the truth.

It took a good ten minutes for Ethan to get his pedal boat maneuvered onto the trailer with the other boats, and he figured his Popsicle had probably melted. As he made his way to the picnic table, he saw just two empty wrappers and Popsicle sticks on the table.

Lindy's back was to him as he neared, and she leaned toward Jerry and talked softly to him. It was a beautiful image, so similar to that of mother and child.

He hadn't lied to her. She *would* make an

excellent mother. He was certain of it. In fact, she'd make an excellent mother for the little boy beside her now.

Ethan stepped slowly toward them, not wanting to break the tender moment.

"This will make you happy," Jerry said, smiling as he handed her a bright yellow daffodil.

Her back trembled, as though she might be crying, or holding back tears. "You know what? You're right," she said, and Ethan heard the heartfelt emotion in her voice. "It does, Jerry. It makes me so very happy. *You* make me happy, more than you could ever know."

"I love you, Mommy."

Ethan's heart pulsed rapidly. Jerry *loved* her. And, Ethan realized with extreme clarity…so did he.

He started to step forward and tell them both how he felt, but he stopped when she continued talking.

"Do you remember who I am, Jerry?" she asked, her voice unsteady and weak from emotion.

Jerry had given her the flower, but he touched the soft petals as he grinned. "You're Miss Lindy."

Lindy's head moved slowly as she nodded, and then she sucked in an audible breath.

"That's right, sweetie, I am. But—but I'm someone else, too, or something else, for you."

Ethan had no idea what she was about to say, but he couldn't wait to hear. Would she tell Jerry that she wanted him to think of her that way, like a mommy, and that she wanted to be there for him always, like a real mother would? Because that's what Ethan thought he wanted, too, for Lindy to be a part of Jerry's life—a real part—and for her to be a part of Ethan's life, too.

He held his breath and waited to see what this woman, who continued to touch him more and more deeply each day, would say to his future son.

"Do you know what else I am, just for you?" Lindy asked.

Jerry's eyebrows dipped, and his lips rolled in as though he was thinking hard about her statement. He shook his head. "No, ma'am."

"Jerry," she said, then inhaled deeply and leaned forward, so that her forehead nearly touched Jerry's, and so that Ethan could no longer see his son's face—but he still heard Lindy's words. "Jerry...I *am* your mommy. Your real mommy, honey. And I love you so very much. I never, *ever* stopped loving you or wanting you. I promise."

The world around Ethan—the trees and the

ground and the bizarre scene unfolding before him—swirled madly, spinning out of control as his mind reeled from the shock of her words. Her confession. His stomach pitched, skin burned. And all he could think was Lindy…

Melinda.

Melinda Sue Flinn.

How? And…why?

But he had no doubt. It all made sense now. The way she'd shown up in Claremont. No job. No place to live.

No *family*.

How had she found her way into Jerry's world? And his? And *why* hadn't he realized who she was, what she wanted? He'd been played…and painfully so. Disgustingly so. *Again*. And by a woman who could keep him from having the boy he wanted so very much. The boy *he* loved!

While he stood there, trying to determine what to say that wouldn't hurt or shock the little guy who'd been hurt enough, he saw Jerry's arms wrap around her.

"You're going to be my mommy!" he said, practically cheering,—and then he spotted Ethan over her shoulder, and his smile brightened. "And *you're* going to be my daddy!"

Still hugging Jerry, she jerked around to see Ethan, her eyes wide with the realization that he'd heard every word she'd said, and knew exactly who she was.

"Melinda." He said the name quietly, pushed from his clamped jaw and his angered soul, and blessedly, Jerry was still too wrapped up in thoughts of a forever mommy and daddy to notice.

"Ethan," she whispered, tears streaming. "I need to tell you— I need to explain."

"Jerry, they're boarding the bus, honey!" Mrs. Bowers called from the back deck.

Jerry tilted forward and squeezed Lindy tightly again. "Bye, Mommy." Then he tilted his head. "Did my flower not make you happy?"

"Oh, yes, sweetie. It did," she said, returning his hug and then whispering against his ear, "You—you always make me happy."

Jerry wiggled out of her arms and then ran straight to Ethan.

Ethan pulled him close, kissed his cheek and thought about how he could save this little boy from the woman who'd fooled them both. "I love you, buddy."

"I love you, too, Daddy," he answered, hugging Ethan and then running toward the rest of his friends, all heading for the bus.

Ethan remained rooted where he stood, anger rippling through him—so much anger that he knew better than to turn around and face the woman who had been lying to him since the day they met.

A moment passed, while he struggled between walking away without speaking and telling her *exactly* what he thought about her deceit.

"I was going to tell you today," she said, her voice so faint it was almost inaudible. He assumed her tears were still falling. But he wouldn't look at her, not now. Not ever. Didn't want to be drawn into, or moved by, any more of her lies.

"I didn't mean for you to hear about it like that," she said, her voice coming across as though she were tortured to speak—as though she were tortured, period—and it was all Ethan could do not to sneer. "But I just had to let him know. Today was so important, because he went on the boat when I knew he was scared. He did that because of us, don't you see? He needs us, both of us. And he can feel it, that I'm his mommy. I know he can. And he sees you as his daddy, Ethan. It's—it's everything I've prayed for."

He shook his head, disbelieving. How could she believe anything about this was an answered prayer? "You," he exhaled, letting it out and fighting to control the fury enough to speak, "You didn't protect him. You stood by, and you let—"

"I didn't, Ethan," she interrupted. "Every time Gil tried to hurt him, I didn't let him. I *always* got between them. He'd hit me, not Jerry. I promise. He never hurt Jerry, not until…"

Not until? "Not until *what*?" He couldn't stop himself; he turned and glared directly at her, crying and pushing at her cheeks to swipe the tears away, and for the briefest moment, he wanted to comfort this woman that he'd actually thought he loved. But this wasn't Lindy. This was Melinda Sue Flinn, and she'd stood by and let a little boy be hurt by his father, just like Ethan's own mother had done to him. "Not until what, Lindy?" he repeated, and then corrected himself. "Melinda?"

"Not until that last night," she whispered. "Gil was giving him his bath, and Jerry stopped splashing, stopped making any noise at all, and I thought—I was so scared—I still don't know what happened behind that locked door before he finally brought Jerry out and threw him at me on the couch." She shook her head, pressed her hands to her eyes. "I was so glad he was alive, and so—so scared that something would happen again where I wouldn't be able to get to him."

Rage tore through him. What had Gil Flinn done to his little boy? "So you *didn't* protect him."

"I couldn't get to him," she said. "It was the only time I couldn't get to him, and so I left. That night. Gil was drinking and passed out… and I left. I went to a shelter. And the next morning, the police came. Gil was dead, and I was arrested. But I didn't do it. You know that now. I *didn't* do it."

Ethan didn't know what he knew. Because *everything* about Lindy Burnett—Melinda Sue Flinn—was a lie.

"And that's why I thought he was afraid of the water, of the boats, but he did that today, with us. He did it, Ethan." She was shaking now, her words coming out in spurts as she tried to get Ethan to understand.

But there was no understanding. Her son— the son he wanted—had been hurt. Maybe she couldn't have gotten to him that night, but how many times before that could she have gotten away from the man she knew was capable of hurting Jerry?

"I am his mother, Ethan. And I love him. I want him. He needs me." She swiped at more tears, and as she did, the flower she'd clutched in one hand snapped in two, the bloom that'd been so beautiful a moment ago plummeting to the ground.

The memory of himself at six years old, buckling to the floor after his father tore his knee apart, pushed through him as distinctly as if it were happening all over again.

No child should ever be hurt by his father. And no mother should ever allow it to happen.

"You'll *never* have him."

Chapter Twelve

"I miss Miss Lindy." Jerry held his fishing pole and frowned at the bobber that had refused to go under since they'd sat beneath this willow tree an hour ago. He'd made the statement at least three times every day Ethan had seen him for the past four weeks. And, as usual, Jerry followed it with words that really gave Ethan a punch to the gut. "I miss my mommy."

"I know, buddy," he said, willing a fish to bite their line, or something else to happen to break the tension that had only seemed to escalate since the court had proclaimed this precious boy as Ethan's son two weeks ago.

Lindy hadn't even shown up in court, nor had she sent any correspondence to be shared at the hearing. According to her attorney, when she'd learned that the assigned judge was known for situational rulings, she'd given up.

Given up. On raising the little boy Ethan knew she loved more than life itself.

Given up…because of Ethan.

"Someone's here," Jerry said, pointing toward the back deck of the store, where a man waved.

"Right. Well, let's go see what he needs. Sound good?"

Jerry nodded but then said, for probably the tenth time today, "Miss Lindy is supposed to do the store. She's really good at it."

"I know, bud. I know." Ethan led him toward the fellow, David Presley, the owner of the bookstore on the town square.

David frowned as they neared. "Still no sign of her?"

The entire town, particularly those at church, knew how Lindy had left, and how Ethan had offered to stay and work at the fishing hole until he had to go back to teach. One reason was that he didn't want Mr. and Mrs. Bowers to be in a bind because of his stupidity. And another was that this was the only place he could think of for Lindy to return to.

And he needed to see her again. Desperately.

"Still no sign of her," he said, while Jerry huffed out a breath beside him.

"I miss Mommy."

David shook his head, and so did Ethan.

Jerry's references to her alternated between Miss Lindy and Mommy, and Ethan didn't correct him on either count. One day he'd figure it out, that Miss Lindy actually was his real mommy.

And if that day came without Ethan finding her and making things right, he feared how much his son would blame him for taking the woman they both loved out of his world.

Because in the month that had transpired since he'd told her she would never have her son, Ethan had plenty of time to realize just how horribly he'd messed up. And he'd tried to find out where she'd gone. But no one knew. And she wouldn't answer her phone.

So he was left with a sad little boy, a new but temporary job at the fishing hole...and a boatload of guilt.

"I'll be praying for you to find her," David said, handing Ethan money for the bucket of minnows he had in hand.

"I appreciate that," Ethan said while David started toward the pond and Jerry walked toward the rear entrance of the store.

"Can I get a Popsicle, Daddy?"

Ethan's heart still thudded hard in his chest every time he called him that, and it ached because he knew how much it'd meant to Lindy when he'd called her mommy. "Sure. Get whatever flavor you want, but wash your hands first, okay?"

"Yes, sir." He disappeared into the store while Ethan looked at the flowers that needed watering and remembered the day he'd walked up to see the most beautiful woman in the world watering those flowers...and claiming his heart.

He'd told her that her past didn't matter to him. Assured her that it wasn't a prison. But it was. It literally *had* been a prison for Lindy, for a crime she hadn't committed. And Ethan hadn't done any better than the jury that had put an innocent woman behind bars. He'd accused and condemned her without considering that she could be telling him the truth. Unlike Ethan's mother, Lindy had done her best to protect her little boy, and Ethan had been so angry—and so immersed in the pain of his own past—that he hadn't believed her.

He needed to beg her forgiveness. And he needed to get his little man's mommy back in his life. But he couldn't find her. Mrs. Bowers said she hadn't revealed where she was going.

He kept thinking about how her life had changed over the past month because of him. She no longer had her job at the fishing hole, and since she'd been living above the sporting goods store, she also didn't have a place to live.

Guilt knifed through him. What if, because of him, she was now homeless?

God, please help me find her. And please, Lord, let her forgive me when I do.

His phone rang, and he saw Candace's number displayed on the screen. Frowning, Ethan answered. "Hey, Candace. Any news?"

"I'm sorry, Ethan. I've tried to find out, but we have no idea where Lindy is. I even tried to send a message through her attorney that you want to talk to her, but he said he won't divulge information about his former client."

"I have to find her."

"I agree you should," Candace said, "but I'm not sure how to go about it."

Jerry exited the store and took a seat at the same wrought iron table where Ethan had watched Lindy enjoy that apple puff pastry.

Ethan stepped to the other end of the deck and lowered his voice. "I've got to go, Candace. I'll keep you posted on whether I find her."

"Okay, and, Ethan?"

"Yeah?"

"I know it's bittersweet now, with everything that ended up happening, but I realized that I never congratulated you on your adoption. Jerry is yours now—whether you find Lindy or not, you do have your son."

He glanced at the little boy he loved, thinking about how sad he'd been since Lindy had left town. "I've wanted that for so long…" He let the word hang, and Candace knew where his mind had gone.

"But you want her to be a part of his life, too."

"Yeah," he admitted. *And mine.*

A car horn sounded, and Jerry glanced to the parking lot. "There's Miss Savvy and Dylan. Is it time for the devo?"

"Must be," Ethan said. He hadn't realized it was that late in the afternoon.

Savvy got out of the car and waved. "You want me to bring him to the B and B after the devo is over?" Since Ethan worked at the fishing hole until five o'clock, Savvy had offered to take Jerry to and from the afternoon devotions at Willow's Haven each day, not only so he could have time learning about God each day, but also so the transition of leaving the new friends he'd made at the children's home would be a little smoother. Candace thought that was important, and Ethan agreed.

"That'd be great," he said while Jerry tossed his Popsicle stick in a trash can and then moved toward Ethan.

"Love you, Daddy," he said, reaching for Ethan.

Ethan leaned toward his son and wrapped his

arms around him to receive the much-needed hug. He loved this kid so much. "I love you, too."

Jerry gave him a little smile before starting to run toward Savvy's car, but paused a short distance away. "Daddy?" he called.

"Yeah, Jerry?" Ethan answered.

"Will you try and find Mommy? I really do miss her."

"I will," he said, unsure how he would keep that promise. Then he silently added, *I miss her, too.*

He watched Jerry climb in the car and waved until Savvy backed up to drive away, while Mrs. Bowers's car came into view in the distance.

Ethan waited on the deck while she parked and held up a hand as she got out of the car and walked directly toward him.

"Catch anything?" she asked, her tone much less friendly toward him than it'd been a month ago. And Mrs. Tingle had actually served him cold cereal every day for the past two weeks. And cold bagels the two weeks before. Clearly the two were not happy with him, and he didn't blame them.

He wasn't very happy with himself.

"We didn't catch a thing," he admitted, spying a used quilt in one of the rocking chairs and moving it to the bin for used ones.

"Pity," she said, "for Jerry." She picked up the watering can and wasted no time filling it with water, then started on the plants, eyeing him as though he should have already done the chore.

No doubt she was still mad. Ethan hadn't attempted to explain his behavior, because nothing warranted the way he'd treated Lindy, and he didn't try now. However, he did tell her the truth. "I've done my best to try to find her and apologize, but she isn't answering her phone, and no one seems to know where she went."

She stopped watering the current plant, propped a hand on her hip and asked, "You keep telling me that you're trying to find her, but you haven't once told me why. *Why* are you trying to find her, Ethan?"

"Like I said, to apologize."

"Mmm-hmm." One side of her mouth tilted down, and she gave him one of those slow nods that implied skepticism.

"I'm telling the truth, Mrs. Bowers."

She huffed out a breath and then placed the watering can on the nearest table. "And is that the only reason you need to find her? To apologize?"

What did she want him to say?

And then he knew.

"No. No, ma'am, it isn't."

Her eyebrows lifted. "Okay then, why *else* do you need to find her?"

"To tell her how I feel."

"Which is?"

"I…think I'd rather say it to her first," he answered.

Mrs. Bowers clapped her hands together. "Well, all right then. I suppose I might be able to help you out, if that's the case."

Ethan moved toward her. "You can help me out? Do you know where she went? All this time, the past four weeks, I've been asking, and you— Do you know where she is?"

"See, that's the thing. You haven't asked the correct question, and I promised I wouldn't tell you anything on my own. But if you asked the correct question, I might be able to give you the correct answer." She lifted a shoulder. "That's the way life is at times. You can't find the answers you need if you aren't asking the right questions."

But she'd lost Ethan. "What? Mrs. Bowers, I've asked you several times over the past week if you knew where she went, and you said you didn't know."

"Well, it wasn't exactly that I didn't know.

It was that she didn't go." She leaned against the deck rail and waited for him to put the pieces together.

And it finally clicked. "She didn't go? You mean she never left? Is she still staying above the sporting goods store?"

"That child came here with hardly any money, no job and no place to live. Where was she going to go? I told her that just because you had ended up being foolish and dim-witted, she didn't need to leave. She should stay with people who cared about her and who wanted to help her. She needed a place to live, and we gave her one. She still has her job, too, as far as I'm concerned, even if she won't come here because she doesn't want to watch you bonding with *her* little boy. So she's been working the back room of the store, keeping things stocked, placing orders and all of that. And, I guess, waiting for you to leave town before she comes out in public again."

"Lindy has been here? This whole time?"

A single nod gave him the answer he wanted.

"Well?" she asked.

"Well, what?" he said, thinking of everything he needed to say to the woman who held his heart.

"Well, what are you waiting for?"

* * *

Lindy prayed that Mr. and Mrs. Bowers would understand when they found her note. She simply couldn't stay in Claremont. Every time she'd go to the fishing hole, she'd remember her time with Jerry and Ethan. She'd think about hearing her son call her Mommy and Ethan Daddy. Ethan would hear that again, often, but she'd never hear her boy say anything again, much less the name she loved.

Mommy.

Ethan was right. She hadn't protected him. She didn't deserve him and couldn't give him the kind of life he needed, the way Ethan could.

Ethan.

She'd hurt him, lied to him, deceived him. She hadn't closed her eyes a single night since that last day without seeing his face, so angry, and hearing his voice, filled with rage.

You'll never have him.

And he was right. She wouldn't. She was glad that Mr. and Mrs. Bowers had offered to let her stay, but it was torturing her very soul to stay where she'd finally made new memories with Jerry. And with Ethan. Staying here only reminded her of the pain. And the loss.

God, I have no idea where I'm going or what I'll do when I get there. Guide me, please. And heal my heart, Lord. Heal me from the pain of losing Jerry. And heal me from the pain of losing Ethan.

She knew God had led her to Claremont to find Jerry. Now she needed Him to lead her to whatever her life should be without her son— though she couldn't imagine her life without her two guys... Jerry and Ethan.

Cotton fields lined both sides of the road between Claremont and Stockville, white tufts as bright as snow. So very white, and so very void of color. Except for one bunch of brilliant yellow up ahead, and as she neared, she recognized the stunning daffodils...just like the one Jerry had picked for her their last day together at the fishing hole.

She slammed on the brakes. Turned the car around. She'd taped the flower together after it had broken and had been drying it. She'd placed it between the pages of the Bible Jolaine had loaned her, and it was still in her room. That Bible held her last gift, last memory, of her son.

She had to go back.

It took twenty minutes to return to the store. She'd left without Mr. Bowers, who was working up front, noticing. Hopefully she could enter and leave again without him seeing and asking her questions that she didn't want to answer.

Where was she going? She didn't know.

Why was she leaving? Because it hurt too much to stay.

Why wasn't she fighting for her son? Because the battle was over, and she'd lost.

But thankfully, Mr. and Mrs. Bowers were nowhere to be seen when she returned. She quietly headed up the stairs, found the Bible and gently removed the precious flower from inside. She cradled it in her palm as she went back down the stairs, turned toward the back door…and saw the man she loved standing in the doorway.

Her heart flipped over in her chest. He looked as beautiful as she remembered—dark hair drawing attention to even darker eyes, a strong jaw, full lips, and a muscled build that said he could protect everyone he cared about. And she knew he would. He would take care of Jerry…forever.

It took a moment to push words past the thick, heavy lump in her throat. "Ethan. I'm… leaving." She struggled to think through why he could be here. "Were you here to see Mr. Bowers? I think he's in the front."

"I thought you'd already left," he said.

"I…did." She lifted her palm, where the tender golden petals rested against her skin. "But I forgot Jerry's flower and—" she swallowed "—I couldn't stand the thought of not having it."

"Lindy, I'm sure he'll pick you more flowers. Lots of them." He spoke the words softly as he moved toward her.

"He'll…" Her hand quivered, and she feared she would drop the precious flower. "How—how would he pick me more?"

Dare she hope? Would Ethan actually let her see her son every now and then?

Please, God.

"I would have come and found you sooner, but I didn't know you were here," he said, still moving closer. Until she could barely breathe. He looked so intent on…something.

What was he going to do? He wasn't like Gil. She was certain of that. Ethan Green would never hit her. He'd never hurt anyone.

But what was he here for now?

"Ethan?"

"I tried to make it a prison," he said, so close now that she could feel his warmth nearing, "but it should be a classroom. It *is* a classroom."

Her mind tripped over his words, but she wasn't following. "I…don't understand."

"It's like you said. Fear says the past is a prison, but God says it's a classroom." He swallowed, the thick cords of his neck pulsing with the action. "When I learned who you were, I didn't treat you the way God would've wanted you treated. I placed you in a prison because of your past, instead of realizing that it was your classroom." He shook his head. "You've been through prison, literally, and every day that you were there was another day you missed out on the joy you deserved. Another day you missed out on being with your son. On being with Jerry."

"Ethan? What are you saying?"

"I'm saying you should have never been away from Jerry. I know you tried to protect him. I believe you, and I should have believed you when you told me before."

She shook her head. "Why should you have believed me? I'd been withholding the truth from you since the day we met. You should hate me. You shouldn't even want to—"

"I love you."

His words halted her midsentence, and she couldn't remember what she'd planned to say. "I— You...love me?"

"I love you, and I'm pretty sure I have for quite some time. And I believe you should raise your son, but…"

"But?"

"But I am hoping—praying—that you'll not only want to be a part of his life—" he placed a finger beneath her chin "—but also a part of mine."

"You…" It was as if she'd forgotten how to communicate. The emotions were too over-whelming.

"I love you, Lindy."

"I love you, too," she whispered.

He smiled. "I was kind of hoping you did." He tilted her chin, brought his mouth to hers and gave her a kiss she'd never forget.

"Mommy and Daddy are kissing!"

They broke the kiss and turned to see Jerry, his blue eyes wide and his hand slapping his mouth against a big grin. Savvy stood behind him shrugging.

"I took him to the B and B, and Mrs. Tingle told me to bring him here, so I did. I didn't re-alize…"

"It's fine," Ethan said, laughing. Then he turned to Jerry. "Do you think you could get used to Mommy and Daddy kissing every now and then?"

Jerry ran across the room and hurled him-self into Ethan's arms, and then he reached for Lindy so that they formed a perfect little cir-cle. He kissed his mommy's cheek, and then his daddy's. "Daddy loves Mommy," he said.

"And Mommy loves Daddy," Lindy confirmed.

And then, just for good measure, she kissed him again, while their little boy giggled and while the world seemed absolutely right.

Epilogue

One year later

"Thank you so much for putting all of this together for us," Lindy said to the two women smiling proudly on the back deck of the fishing hole's cottage. "After my grandmother passed away, and since I never knew my parents, I didn't think I would ever have a real wedding."

Jolaine Bowers wrapped an arm around Annette Tingle. "Can't imagine anything we'd have rather been doing. Besides, we're the ones who set all of this in motion, so it was only fitting that we help y'all celebrate right. I always knew this place would make a beautiful wedding venue."

"True, true," Annette said, peering out over the wedding guests enjoying the reception, which included fishing and pedal boats.

Ethan had clearly overheard the conversation and was laughing as he climbed the deck steps. "Yeah, I don't know what would've happened to us without you two."

"Me either," Jolaine said, and Lindy, giggling, suspected the lady actually believed that.

Ethan moved near Lindy and wrapped an arm around his wife, sending a wave of goose bumps up her arms.

"Think I'll always have that effect on you?" he asked, running a finger over the sensitive flesh.

"I shouldn't have told you about that," she said, "and then you wouldn't know to look for it."

"I'd have figured it out. And I think it's adorable." He lifted a shoulder. "And it makes me feel a little powerful."

Annette chuckled, and then cleared her throat, probably to remind the newlyweds that they weren't the only ones on the deck. "Look at all of the Willow's Haven kids. They're having so much fun!"

"They sure are, and it was a wonderful idea for you to invite them all," Jolaine said. "And only fitting, since y'all are volunteering there for the summer."

"We plan to do that every year," Lindy said.

Ethan nodded. "I suspect it'll be the highlight of our year."

"Maybe one of them," Annette said, "because I'm thinking you'll have many highlights in your years now, thanks to that little guy. In fact, I'd say he's probably making a moment to remember right now."

Jerry, in drenched khaki shorts and a white dress shirt—his ring bearer uniform—ran toward the deck. "Daddy! Mommy! Everybody is swimming and splashing, even with their clothes on. Can I swim, too? Even in my clothes?"

Ethan grinned. "It looks like you already have been," he pointed out.

"Nah, this is from splashing. They have lifejackets, and I'll wear one."

"What do you think?" Ethan asked Lindy.

"As long as you wear a life jacket," she said.

"Awesome!" Jerry started to dash away, but then turned. "Maybe next time you can swim with me?"

"Maybe so," Ethan said, smiling at the boy heading toward the pier.

They watched James Bowers help Jerry put on a red life jacket, and then they saw their son run to the end of the pier and jump in.

"He's come so far," Lindy said, emotion filling each word.

"Yes, he has," Ethan marveled.

"A shame you can't swim with him like he wanted," Annette said softly.

Lindy overheard the comment and glanced at her husband, who had a mischievous twinkle in those chocolate eyes.

"What do you think?" she asked.

"It's *your* wedding dress."

She smiled, suddenly overwhelmed by how much had happened over the past year. She had her son in her life again, and she had the most amazing husband. God had definitely heard and answered each and every prayer. "Yes, it's my wedding dress," she said, "but I'll only need to wear it once."

"Well, all right then," he said, scooping her into his arms and running toward the water.

"Look at my mommy and daddy!" Jerry yelled, his eyes wide as Ethan sprinted down the pier with Lindy, her laughter filling the air as she bounced against his chest.

And Lindy plunged into the water, safe in her husband's arms, with their son cheering nearby and her heart absolutely and totally filled to the brink with an overabundance of love.

* * * * *

Dear Reader,

Lindy could have remained confined by her past, by her fear that she hadn't protected her son and that he wouldn't recover his father's abuse. But God doesn't mean for us to be trapped by the past. If that was what He intended, why send His son? He intended for us to accept His grace and forgiveness—forgiveness not only from Him, but also from ourselves.

Are you using your past as a prison or a classroom? Learn from mistakes and move forward. Forgive yourself, because God already has.

As always, I welcome prayer requests from readers. Write to me at Renee Andrews, PO Box 8, Gadsden, AL 35902, or through email at renee@reneeandrews.com, and I will gladly lift your requests to our Heavenly Father in prayer.

And keep up with me, my family, my books and my devotions on my Facebook page at www.Facebook.com/AuthorReneeAndrews.

Blessings in Christ,
Renee

Get 2 Free Books,
Plus 2 Free Gifts—
just for trying the Reader Service!

Love Inspired® SUSPENSE

LIS17R2

Get 2 Free Books,
Plus 2 Free Gifts—
just for trying the Reader Service!

HARLEQUIN
HEARTWARMING™

YES! Please send me 2 FREE Harlequin® Heartwarming™ Larger-Print novels and my 2 FREE mystery gifts (gifts worth about $10 retail). After receiving them, if I don't wish to receive any more books, I can return the shipping statement marked "cancel." If I don't cancel, I will receive 4 brand-new larger-print novels every month and be billed just $5.49 per book in the U.S. or $6.24 per book in Canada. That's a savings of at least 19% off the cover price. It's quite a bargain! Shipping and handling is just 50¢ per book in the U.S. and 75¢ per book in Canada.* I understand that accepting the 2 free books and gifts places me under no obligation to buy anything. I can always return a shipment and cancel at any time. The free books and gifts are mine to keep no matter what I decide.

161/361 IDN GLWT

Name   (PLEASE PRINT)

Address   Apt. #

City   State/Prov.   Zip/Postal Code

Signature (if under 18, a parent or guardian must sign)

Mail to the **Reader Service:**
IN U.S.A.: P.O. Box 1341, Buffalo, NY 14240-8531
IN CANADA: P.O. Box 603, Fort Erie, Ontario L2A 5X3

Want to try two free books from another line?
Call 1-800-873-8635 today or visit www.ReaderService.com.

* Terms and prices subject to change without notice. Prices do not include applicable taxes. Sales tax applicable in N.Y. Canadian residents will be charged applicable taxes. Offer not valid in Quebec. This offer is limited to one order per household. Books received may not be as shown. Not valid for current subscribers to Harlequin Heartwarming Larger-Print books. All orders subject to approval. Credit or debit balances in a customer's account(s) may be offset by any other outstanding balance owed by or to the customer. Please allow 4 to 6 weeks for delivery. Offer available while quantities last.

Your Privacy—The Reader Service is committed to protecting your privacy. Our Privacy Policy is available online at www.ReaderService.com or upon request from the Reader Service.

We make a portion of our mailing list available to reputable third parties that offer products we believe may interest you. If you prefer that we not exchange your name with third parties, or if you wish to clarify or modify your communication preferences, please visit us at www.ReaderService.com/consumerschoice or write to us at Reader Service Preference Service, P.O. Box 9062, Buffalo, NY 14240-9062. Include your complete name and address.

HOMETOWN HEARTS ♥

YES! Please send me **The Hometown Hearts Collection** in Larger Print. This collection begins with 3 FREE books and 2 FREE gifts in the first shipment. Along with my 3 free books, I'll also get the next 4 books from the Hometown Hearts Collection, in LARGER PRINT, which I may either return and owe nothing, or keep for the low price of $4.99 U.S./ $5.89 CDN each plus $2.99 for shipping and handling per shipment*. If I decide to continue, about once a month for 8 months I will get 6 or 7 more books, but will only need to pay for 4. That means 2 or 3 books in every shipment will be FREE! If I decide to keep the entire collection, I'll have paid for only 32 books because 19 books are FREE! I understand that accepting the 3 free books and gifts places me under no obligation to buy anything. I can always return a shipment and cancel at any time. My free books and gifts are mine to keep no matter what I decide.

262 HCN 3432 462 HCN 3432

Name	(PLEASE PRINT)	
Address		Apt. #
City	State/Prov.	Zip/Postal Code

Signature (if under 18, a parent or guardian must sign)

Mail to the **Reader Service:**

IN U.S.A.: P.O. Box 1867, Buffalo, NY. 14240-1867
IN CANADA: P.O. Box 609, Fort Erie, Ontario L2A 5X3

READERSERVICE.COM

Manage your account online!

- Review your order history
- Manage your payments
- Update your address

*We've designed the
Reader Service website
just for you.*

Enjoy all the features!

- Discover new series available to you, and read excerpts from any series.
- Respond to mailings and special monthly offers.
- Browse the Bonus Bucks catalog and online-only exculsives.
- Share your feedback.

Visit us at:

ReaderService.com

RS16R